Man's Illegal Life

Man's Illegal Life

A Novel of Crime...
Set in London, 1722

Keith Heller

CHARLES SCRIBNER'S SONS
NEW YORK

First published in the United States by Charles Scribner's Sons 1985.

Copyright © Keith Heller 1984

Library of Congress Cataloging in Publication Data

Heller, Keith.
    Man's illegal life.

    I. Title.
PS3558.E47614M3   1985   813'.54   84-23604
ISBN 0-684-18299-8

1 3 5 7 9 11 13 15 17 19   H/C   20 18 16 14 12 10 8 6 4 2

Printed in the United States of America.

The very sinking fears they have had of the plague hath brought the plague and death upon many. Some by the sight of a coffin in the streets have fallen into a shivering, and immediately the disease has assaulted them; and Sergeant Death hath arrested them, and clapt to the doors of their houses upon them, from whence they have come forth no more till they have been brought to their graves.

Thomas Vincent,
God's Terrible Voice in the City, (1667)

The quotations in Chapter 6 are taken from the following: Dr Nathaniel Hodges, *Loimologia* (English translation published in 1720); Thomas Vincent, *God's Terrible Voice in the City*, 1667; William Boghurst, *Loimographia*, 1666; and Daniel Defoe, *A Journal of the Plague Year*, 1722. The quotations in Chapter 7 are the author's own.

For Llyr and Felisa
who sustain me
through my own plagues.

A Note on the Watch

In the first half of the eighteenth century London was probably the most dangerous city on earth. Gangs of thieves and beggars, prostitutes and bullies, lunatics and murderers made a battleground of the streets for nobleman and commoner alike. Of London, Samuel Johnson wrote:

> 'Prepare for death, if here at night you roam,
> And sign your will before you sup from home.'

Corruption and negligence were the order of the day, and the legal system was more notorious for its brutality than for its effectiveness. In the midst of this chaos, one astounding fact stands clear: there were no police.

Instead, London had to depend upon the centuries-old system of the parish watch. Loosely supervised by the constable, who hired them, and paid out of parish funds, the watchmen patrolled the streets from sunset to sunrise 'to apprehend all rogues, vagabonds, and night-walkers, and make them give an account of themselves' (Blackstone, I, 9, IV). Ridiculed by the very people they were meant to serve, the watchmen were still the first line of defence in the war of the streets. Many of them were old, decrepit, infirm of body and mind, disorganized, indifferent, sometimes criminal themselves. And for those few who were more able and more dedicated, the work must have seemed doubly thankless and futile against the crime and violence that overran the streets.

There is no record of the watchmen's ever having had any lasting effect on the lawless conditions of eighteenth-century London. But they were there.

Keith Heller

CHAPTER 1

Through the fog George Man could just make out the sign over the alehouse across the street: 'Drunk for a penny, dead-drunk for twopence.'

The rain had fallen sporadically throughout the night, only to give way at dawn to a bone-numbing damp. The mud of the streets was thick and spotted with pools. In front of the grocer's next to the alehouse a child lay asleep in the mire, his forearms thrown across his face.

Man sipped his burning coffee and looked lazily round the small shop. He was alone, except for Hawkins, the proprietor—a slow, shapeless bulk of a man—who was sitting mumbling over yesterday's news-sheet. Man was always the first customer; by now, Hawkins had got into the habit of opening up an hour earlier to accommodate him. The two men had known each other for well over ten years. Making his way home at sunrise, Man would step in to find a coffee with a drop of rum and a penny slice of bread waiting for him on the table at the shop's only window. He had always suspected Hawkins of spying out of the door to watch for him, but he had never been able to catch him at it. Their greeting never varied.

'An early morning.'

'Yes, a long night.'

Over the years, neither of them had ever noticed anything incongruous about the exchange. It had gradually become a comforting tradition.

Man dipped the last bit of bread in his coffee. His regular September cold was getting worse. His head felt heavy and dull. Bending over to knock out his pipe against the scarred floor, he could feel the pressure building behind his cheekbones. He filled his pipe from a ragged black-leather bag that he pulled from beneath his greatcoat. Even the coarse tobacco felt chilled and stiff. He lit it from a stub of candle, and soon the window was covered with shifting blue smoke. The pipe had that oddly satisfying tang that illness always gave to it.

Outside in the street a man pulled a two-wheeled hand-cart stacked with strips of brittle leather down the street, labouring against the drag of the mud. A minute later another passed in the opposite direction with a porter's knot on his back, the loop slipped half over his eyes. London was waking.

Man sat back and thought with pleasure of home. By this time, Sarah would be up and busy preparing some meat and tea for his return. Then, while he ate, she would begin warming the bed with coals. They would not talk much. After eighteen years of marriage there was no need.

Hawkins brought over the coffee and sat down heavily across from him. The owner rubbed his palms roughly across his broad face. His thick forearms were matted with unwashed hair.

'Uncle Hoole was in last night.'

'I've not seen him this past week. Where is he working?'

'The upper end of Drury Lane. He wants to see you.'

'What is it?'

'Well, then, I can't say.' He massaged his jaw with knotted fingers and looked closely at Man's quiet face. 'You know Uncle. Nothing much excites him.'

Man watched the boy in front of the grocer's turn over in his sleep and huddle closer to the building. He grimaced. Had better not mention it to Sarah. Somehow, even with the coffee and the rum, he felt colder.

'I remind me how, back in 'fifteen, during the troubles, the worst of it, how Uncle comes in here of a darkest night and sits down for a glass, as nice as nice, and him with his arm near broke in quarters.' He grunted and wagged his great head. 'Never so much as a change o' face on him.'

Man thought, not for the first time, of how much Hawkins's voice made him think of the trundling of barrels over the hollow floors of his father's brewery. He had carried that memory with him for almost forty years now—that, and the sweet refreshing scent of new ale, and the sparkling foam.

His pipe had gone out. He rapped the dottle loose against the caked sole of his boot. Hawkins offered his own greasy pouch.

'Aye,' said Man, 'there's many of us remember those times. The wounds of it lie open still.'

'But you, Sir, take it harder, if I may say so. Harder anyways than Uncle Hoole.'

'He's somewhat newer at it.'

'True.'

Man thought back to his own early years, of the long succession of bands roving the streets, wild as wolves: the Hectors, the Scourers, the Nickers, the Hawcubites, the Mohawks. Every week brought a new plague of them; and now it was continuing, only worse.

The door opened and let in a palsied old woman, bent almost double, wrapped in a transparent shawl. A mass of cold and smoke congealed about her. She stumbled her way towards a table at the back of the shop.

As he stood up, Hawkins tapped Man's table with a chipped fingernail.

'Well, then, if you see him or no is yours. He told me nothing. But I will say this. Even old Hoole seemed somehow bothered some. 'Feared, almost.'

He moved himself laboriously over to the old woman's table.

Taylor Hoole was older than Man, in his late fifties. He was a contemplative, inward sort of man whose parchment-skinned body seemed never quite wholly present before you. Man liked him, he liked to savour his long silences. Hoole was the kind of man who would insist that he felt at home only in the convivial atmosphere of the coffee-house; but, once he was there, surrounded by his friends and their drink and smoke and talk, he would fall back into a listening posture, the thin lids of his eyes lowered. At such times he would appear almost lifeless.

He had started on the watch much later in life than had Man, perhaps only ten or twelve years ago. He must have been then about Man's age now. No one could say with certainty what he had done before.

Man stood in the street, feeling the cold pinch at his nose. There were more people now, hurrying to the shops, to the markets. Struggling through the slush, they looked worn and tired. A woman with a basket of gloves went by, muttering to herself. A man with a pork haunch over his shoulder that, with the uneven footing, unbalanced him at every other step.

Man stood in indecision. The chilled wet night had not helped his chest, which now seemed unable to expand fully. He thought of his wife, of steaming black tea and still-warm bread.

He stepped carefully across the street and stooped down over the sleeping boy. Gently he prodded him awake.

'Do you belong here, my lad?'

The boy looked to be less than ten years old. The shape of the bones showed beneath the pallid skin. In general appearance he was indistinguishable from the countless wayward children abandoned among the close streets of London.

He awoke as if he were being forced to leave behind something warm and safe.

'No, Sir, but the grocer, Sir, he sometimes has a touch of work that needs doing . . .'

Man looked into the troubled eyes, then away. He

reached into his pocket for a coin.

'Take this, and with it, a message. You are to go and tell my wife that I have been delayed. Stay awake, now.' He lifted the boy to his feet and straightened his shoulders, dismayed to feel how light and skeletal he was. Man thrust his face towards the boy's. The fog of their breaths mingled.

'Do you know what lane this is, then?'

He guessed that the boy knew the narrow streets better than he himself, but more by sight than by name. And he was still sunk in the lethargy of a cold sleep. As Man spoke, the boy roused himself, proud to be entrusted with such an important chore.

'Foster Lane, Sir, is it not?'

'Correct. Now, follow this up into Noble Street until you come into White Cross Street. That will take you up to Old Street.'

The boy blew on his small hands that looked wrinkled and fragile.

'Turn you right into Old Street and continue until you come to Ironmonger Row on your left. There is a brewery on the corner, remember. In that street, there is a bake-shop on the right-hand, and above that you will find my rooms. Can you mind all that?'

After repeating the directions and the message twice, the boy set off up the middle of the street, awkward with sleepiness and hunger. Man knew that he himself would, for part of his way, be following a parallel course. He could have accompanied the boy, but that would have hurt his young pride.

Man turned to walk in the opposite direction, his hands thrust into his threadbare greatcoat. For a moment he thought sorrowfully of how Sarah would take the boy in and try to revive him with food and affection. She would probably even run down for a bowl of scalded milk. The boy might even be there still when he came home later.

Man walked without hurrying. He knew that Hoole never went to bed until ten in the morning, preferring, as most of them did, to stop somewhere first for a coffee and some bread. No rum for Hoole, though; he never drank spirits.

What could it be that would have disturbed even the implacable Uncle Hoole? They had worked together often, under some of the most vicious circumstances imaginable, and Man had never known him to quail. Two years before, in the dark maelstrom of Wapping, they had routed a houseful of desperate thieves and, at one point, Hoole had had to pull him out from under three of the biggest. What was it that had now brought him to seek out Man?

He turned into Cheapside and followed it a short distance to Blowbladder Street, recording the sights and sounds and odours from the shambles there and wondering how many of the butchers still held to tradition by mischievously inflating their wares by means of pipes. As he passed into St Martin's-le-Grand and Aldersgate, the city streets began to warm themselves with the bustle of traffic and business. A fruiterer was laying out his merchandise, turning the most glossy sides upward. At the corner of Bull and Mouth Street, two fanmakers were comparing the quality of their newest work. Through the open door of a glass-seller's escaped a sudden sharp crash. It was always a never-failing surprise to Man to walk the streets by day and contrast the atmosphere with that with which he was more familiar: the sightless depths of the streets enclosed by night, darker even than the darkness of the country, a reversed world where nothing could be known, nothing was safe and normal. He had been a night-walker for twenty-seven of his forty-three years, and he still marvelled at the twin transformations which took place at sunsetting and sunrising.

He bore left at the Charterhouse. The fog had broken, but the sun was still only a pale silver disc without heat. If anything, the cold weighed even more heavily on the air and penetrated the cloth across his back. The sky to the north held promise of more rain.

Taylor Hoole lived in a cramped garret near St John's Gate. From his single window he could view the massive crouching remnant of the medieval monastery. He had been suspected of forgoing his day's sleep in order to watch the gradual shifting of light over its rough uneven stones.

And, in fact, even though the day was practically sunless, Man found him at the window in a plain chair with three legs which he was constantly obliged to lean up against the wall. Man had long since tired of wondering why he never made the effort to have it repaired.

'I saw your coming.'

Man sat down in the other chair. He gathered his coat in his lap, as the room had no fire.

'I was at Hawkins's this morn.'

Man studied him. Taylor Hoole was a gaunt, angular man with a profile that most found difficult to forget. The line of the jaw was not so much determined as immovable. The eyes were deep-set, haunted, and the nose long and thin. His sharp body caused his clothes to hang in a misshapen cluster, as though from a slack line. He had always the nervous habit of pressing the tips of his bony fingers into his closed eyes so forcefully that it appeared to others to be dangerous.

'You were watching in upper Drury Lane last night, I understand.'

Hoole was always slow to respond, as if each word were too ponderous to bring forth.

'The first time in months it was. We were down in Little Knightrider and Old Fish Streets previously.'

'Who was with you, then?'

'You know, I believe, only Edward Scripture. A few others.'

'Was that good man in Drury Lane?'

'The two of us, yes.'

Most of the watch were confined to a single parish, often to a limited number of contiguous streets. But some, depending upon need and upon their personal acquaintance with individual constables, transferred themselves randomly from place to place. Usually, these were the few who were well-regarded for their experience and resourcefulness.

'Constable Legge had report of a crew of anglers who were to be working there late. We found but one, too young he was to concern us much.'

Hoole was peering out of the window with that peculiar intentness which is common in those who are accustomed most to deep night. Man moved slightly in his chair and wished for something hot and strong to drink.

The growing traffic in the street sent a confused murmur up towards the two men through the crooked window.

'We were taking the lad to the watch-house, when I happened to note one house that struck me as different in appearance, strange somehow.' He paused, then emphasized his words. 'Disbelieve, Sir, if you will, but the very sight of that house rang somehow false to me.'

'You have always seemed to me more enthusiastic than most, Mr Hoole,' said Man, trusting that the other would not notice the gentle irony.

Hoole's fingertips were once more against his eyes. Man had the sudden impression that Hoole was no longer fully aware of the presence of his visitor, a feeling that was further confirmed as Hoole opened his eyes into a numb unblinking stare. He was back in the previous night, immersed in solitude and shadow, confronting an indecipherable enigma.

'There was nothing specifically unusual about the
appearance of the house,' he continued in a voice now
lacking all inflection. 'We have all, in our time, beheld
such empty and disused dwellings—the windows shut by
plain deal boards, the door secured by a heavy padlock,
the official sign-board indicating vacancy. Such sights are
not uncommon in this city today. I have myself passed
hundreds by with hardly a glance. No, Sir, this was not
typical. I stood perhaps a quarter of an hour before it,
trying to resolve the mysteriousness which I somehow
sensed. Will you scoff, Sir, if I should use the word
"malevolence" before you?'

Man chose to make no kind of answer. He left such
metaphysical speculations to others. To him, the merely
human was too regularly obscure enough.

He watched as his friend began to stir uneasily in his
precarious chair. At this point, he wondered, did Hoole
even notice the added chill that had started to invade the
room and turn the air a dim blue? Outside, the faint light
grew weaker and the wind increased.

'I speak of this as a partial explanation of my sub-
sequent actions. I had some time before sent Mr Scripture
on his way to the watch-house with the boy, saying that I
wished to remain in the street on watch for others of the
band. I am afraid that I shall soon have to beg that man's
pardon for that deviation from the truth.'

Taylor Hoole appeared as near to squirming as his
wavering chair would allow. Man had always thought his
friend laboured under a conscience that was unnaturally
sensitive.

'In short,' Hoole went on, 'I forced an entry into the
place. I used my staff to pry open one of the boards laid
across the window. The window itself was not fastened. I
shone my lanthorn inward and called out softly once or
twice. Happily, the hour was very late, and there was
none in the street to observe me. Yet you know, of course,

that we have some leave to enter a man's house, if we should suspect something to be amiss.'

'Of course.'

Both knew that this was not strictly true. Without a warrant, the constable or his officers had to be able to show that a felon was in the house, that entry was denied, and that such denial followed proper demand and notice. Yet these regulations had often to be ignored in practice.

Hoole seemed to feel the need to justify himself still further.

'The band of anglers had, after all, been notorious in the street for some time. You know, Sir, as well as I the low character of that area. I have before known such gangs to house themselves within such premises. But when I stepped through on to the window-seat and into the parlour, I sensed that the house was indeed empty of life.'

At these words Hoole faltered for a moment, as if a new realization had just occurred to him.

'I reduced the light from my lanthorn and surveyed the room. Everything was covered with a visible layer of dust. I thought then that the house must not have been occupied for a month or more. The dining-room across the front hall was in a similar condition. I remember that, in ascending the staircase, I struck with my leg the open door of a low cupboard in the wall. Such are used for the storing of the bedtime candles, are they not?'

Man nodded.

'It was, as I say, open and had been emptied of its contents. On the first floor, I found two plain drawing-rooms, sparsely furnished. The air throughout was very close. The bedrooms are on the second floor, and the bed linen appeared stale and undisturbed. I hesitated to search the garret, but it was so small that a mere glance told me it had been long unused. Even so, on its floor could be seen the remains of a large number of candle-

ends. I must tell you, Sir, that at this time my nerve began
to fail me. The darkness and the silence of the house
worked upon me terribly. I had, at one and the same
moment, the sensation that the entirety of the house was
devoid of any breathing soul save for myself—and yet that
I was not there completely alone.

'At the back of the front hall was a door from which a
short staircase descends direct to a large kitchen with
walls of whitened plaster. There were also the usual open
fireplaces, stone sink, cistern, and pump. The walls
seemed to expand in the uncertain light of my lamp.'

He stopped for breath. Man knew that he was unused
to such lengthy speech.

'It was in the kitchen that I found him. He was bound
by strong fetters to an upright chair, which he had
evidently flung over upon its side in his struggles to free
himself. His legs were tied to those of the chair, his arms
behind. A thick cloth had been forced into his mouth and
around his head. An old man, but obviously once hearty.
I say "once," for now was he horribly drawn and
emaciated, the flesh hanging loosely from his bones, his
clothes almost engulfing him. The eyes were open still,
bulging and staring in profound terror. The line of the
mouth about the cloth had been frozen in that straining
grimace which we sometimes see on those unfortunates in
the streets who have choked to death on their own
vomitus. In the neck, the cords stood out in a manner
that was painful to behold.'

It was at this moment that the wind chose to hurl the
first icy drops of rain against the loosened window-glass.

What is it, Man asked himself, about this story—or
about Taylor Hoole's telling of it—that seems still
incomplete? All of the details were evidently clear, even
the atmosphere had been rendered in the retelling with a
care uncharacteristic of the man—yet the design, the
reason, remained hidden. Was it because that, behind

the peculiar hideousness of it, lay no comprehensible pattern whatsoever?

Man rejected this, automatically. He had always held that every mortal action resulted from a motivation that was fully consistent with itself, no matter how idiosyncratic or even mad it might appear to others. And, with time, the reason could be discovered and understood, if not forgiven.

Hoole had now turned to face Man directly. His bony hands clasped and unclasped convulsively, and his breathing sounded hollow.

'I left the man as he was and duly notified Constable Legge, after having boarded up the window once more. My duties took me elsewhere. To my uncertain knowledge, the appropriate coroner and justices are even now progressing with their inquiries. You are as familiar as I with the procedures of our superiors.'

He leant forward, his face for once tensed and feverish.

'You realize, Sir, that the man had been deliberately and methodically starved to death!'

Hoole sat back in utter emotional exhaustion. Man waited for some minutes before speaking.

'Do we know his name?'

'I am not, as I am sure you must know, now even indirectly involved. Such levels of authority are not open to such as us.' He spoke with some of the bitterness and exasperation which they all felt at times. 'But, after watch ended this morning, I did betake myself to a coffee-shop in St Martin's Lane which I know to be frequented by one of the coroner's minor assistants. The man's name was Geoffrey Stannard. He was known to have owned that same house in Drury Lane for well over fifty years, although to my knowledge he had only recently taken up his residence there.'

'Did you yourself see or talk to any who live in the street?'

'It was quite late, Sir, when I came away from the house. I saw no one, save for the usual scattering of vagrants and beggars asleep in the corners. As for the other houses, we both know the occupation of many in that area. The ladies had by then retired, for it was bitter cold. And I felt obliged to inform the officers as soon as possible.'

He looked a bit cowed as he spoke. Man could well imagine his desire to hurry from the scene of the murder. The streets themselves took on a sinister enough tone, deserted in the dark.

'Did your acquaintance from the coroner's supply anything beyond the man's name?'

'He said the man Stannard had been long known and well-respected in the community. Some eighty years of age, by the clerk's own reckoning. Mr Stannard had been, it is reported, for some while quite a success in business ventures—of exactly what nature, I know not—but he had lately suffered a severe financial reversal. As I think on it, the interior of the house, though orderly enough, was hardly and cheaply furnished, even for the low style of such houses in Drury Lane. The coroner's assistant— his name is Roger Petticrew—informs me that Constable Legge's cursory examination of the house suggests that nothing of value seems to have been removed.'

'So the murder was not done for gain.'

'Unless something small but valuable had been taken which others would not think to miss.'

'Indeed, something only Mr Stannard himself—now silenced—could have wanted.'

Both men sat without speaking, as the rain began to slant against the window with growing insistence.

'Does Mr Petticrew know of any surviving family?' asked Man.

'There seems small hope of that. The gentleman was quite aged, and a glance at the records has shown that he was unmarried.'

Abruptly, Man found his mind straying from the conversation. He wondered, with a sense of anxiety which surprised him, if the beggar boy had safely reached Ironmonger Row and how much of a fuss Sarah was making over him. He would by no means be the first—or, most probably, the last—lost child to be coddled and treasured by his wife. Man thought guiltily of the reduced style of life to which his work subjected her: days of tending to him as he slept or rested, nights of wakeful sleeping alone in a too-quiet house, and always the incessant worry about his walking through the dark and fearful streets. She had her friends, of course, in the neighbourhood; if only she had someone to be more often with her in the home . . .

Hoole stood up, as if he had just come to a private decision, and braced his chair more firmly against the wall. He moved to a far corner of the room, bent down, and carried back a large wooden box. This he set on the floor in front of Man's feet. All was done wordlessly and with no expression on his face.

The box was filled almost to overflowing with a jumble of inexpensive books and pamphlets. Most of them looked to be much handled. They were obviously not the kind of works on metaphysics and theology which Man knew his friend most often favoured.

Hoole had perched himself once more in his chair and turned to gaze out through the film of rain coating the window. Man took this as an invitation to browse. As he ran his eye over the assorted texts, he could not help feeling that here was a part of Hoole's character at which Man himself could never have guessed. He recognized none of the titles: *Loimologia, Short Discourse Concerning Pestilential Contagion, A Journal of the Plague Year, The Late Dreadful Plague at Marseilles Considered, A Brief Journal of What Passed in the City of*

Marseilles While It Was Afflicted with the Plague. There were scores of others, most of them thin and poorly printed.

Man looked at the other in some confusion.

Hoole spoke hurriedly, eager to explain.

'I have, by chance, been interesting myself in this subject for this past year. The obvious connections with the tenets of our faith have long intrigued me. There is, too,' he faltered momentarily, 'something of a personal interest . . . But the fact is, Sir, that the circumstances of last night appeared at once to me as distinctly reminiscent of what I have encountered in my reading. I refer primarily to the complete shutting-up of the house from without and the enforced deprivation of its inhabitants. I believe it was such similarity that first subtly awakened my suspicions about the place.'

Man could not keep an obvious tone of scepticism from his voice. He had always trusted in Hoole's judgement, but he had also tended to feel somewhat uneasy in the presence of his friend's often imaginative theorizing.

'May we not, Mr Hoole, ascribe such likeness to common coincidence? Surely these associations belong to the distant past.'

Hoole waved an impatient hand down towards the box that lay between them.

'You will know, Sir, that most of these date from no further than five years past and many are the products of this year. In some ways, these matters are more alive to us now than at any other time in the past half-century. I am told that Constable Legge, too—a most conscientious Christian—has also remarked upon this feature.'

'Yet you surely do not mean to tell me that Mr Stannard's death is the first evidence of a fresh visitation.'

Hoole considered this for a space.

'I do not think I can say for myself with any certainty whether I believe that is so or whether he met his death at the hands of an outright murderer. I note now only the peculiarities of the situation in which I found him. This alone is what has bemused me for these seven or eight hours.'

Man suddenly felt his weariness. The traffic outside in the street flowed regularly past beneath an unflagging rain that saturated and blurred the air. His cold had clogged his head, preventing him from knowing his own thoughts clearly. He now realized, too, how hungry and thirsty he had become, and how desperately he wanted to smoke a pipe.

The other man was also spent, possibly more from emotional than physical strain. He seemed to sink within himself, his fingers at his eyes, his arms trembling slightly.

'You cannot know the gloom of that darkened house, as neither of us can know the dread of that awful time past. Yet I am older than you, Sir, and I have perhaps heard more from friends and relations of what occurred in those fearful days.'

He looked up, his cheekbones blotched by the pressure of his palms.

'It may be that my interest stems from the fact that I am one of those who came into this world in that very year of which we speak—sixteen sixty-five—the year of the Great Plague.'

CHAPTER 2

Man had been right.

He was sitting at last in his favourite corner chair with a thick blanket across his lap, savouring his third pipe in a row, watching the boy at the table. Toby Childers— seven, mother dead, father gone—was small for his age, so small that Sarah had had to perch him on top of their highest chair and upon an added pile of newspapers and magazines, of which her husband was an incurable collector. The boy was huddled over yet another cup of hot milk with coffee; the remains of egg and bread lay on a plate near his elbow. He was wrapped round in a long sheet, while Sarah sat across from him, mending his shirt and humming a light melody.

Man looked with tenderness at his wife's round, florid face and her solid, comfortable presence. He was tired, but not sleepy. He could go for days with very little sleep, against the protests of his wife, particularly when something unusual had caught his attention.

The story of Geoffrey Stannard's death had interested him as much as it had Taylor Hoole, though Man's reactions were less volatile and emotional. He looked upon any such mystery as being the inevitable last act in an individual human drama, the expression of unknown but ultimately recognizable fears and desires. As sincere a Christian as any, he still had no patience with the popular notion of divine intervention in the daily affairs of the world.

Man had come away from Hoole's with as much information as his friend had to give. He had left him slumped in his unstable chair, paging through a crumpled pamphlet, still so excited that Man feared the onset of a fever. He had politely declined Hoole's offer to lend him some books from the box.

He laid his head back and closed his eyes, lulled by the restful sounds which filled the room: the boy's regular slurping, his wife's unending song, the gurgle of his pipe. A fine rain continued to lash against the window.

But why was Hoole so especially disturbed by the incident? Man knew that this was hardly the first victim whom his friend had found murdered; nor, as a watchman of some thirteen years' experience, could he yet be so profoundly impressed by the unpredictable atrocities of the night-streets. And what lay behind his more than academic devotion to plague-literature and his insistence on some kind of connection? To Man, too, the circumstances of Stannard's death seemed a bit bizarre, but surely open to a variety of less fanciful interpretations.

Yet how much, if anything, did Man really know about Taylor Hoole's life before his friend's joining the watch? Today, for example, had been the first Man had heard of Hoole's exact age. How much more was there to learn?

The boy had finished his milk and was beginning to nod himself to sleep over the empty cup. Sarah kept on sewing, stealing glances at the boy and smiling maternally. Man tucked his blanket about his thighs and reached for the hot drink that his wife always prepared for him when he was worsening for a serious cold. His head felt fuzzy.

Of course, that there were undeniable similarities between the way in which Stannard had been killed and certain measures practised during the last visitation was evident enough. Man had had time to consider this aspect as he had walked home along Old Street. The enforced shutting-up of houses had been then regarded as the most effective method of containing the spread of the disease. Naturally, Man himself had no first-hand recollections — he had not been born until fourteen years later — but he could remember vividly his father's and mother's descriptions of London during those terrible months, a memory made all the more merciless by the Great Fire which had followed in the very next year. How often had he walked with his father through the crowded streets, gazing with awe and fear at the sites reconstructed by his father's melancholy voice: the great burial pit in the churchyard of Aldgate parish and that in Finsbury, in the parish of Cripplegate, under the soil of which young George had imagined the thousands of restless bones; the house in Swan Alley, passing from Goswell Street into St John

Street, in which fire had consumed everything, but had left the diseased bodies of the dead untouched; and the Pied Bull Inn along the road to Islington, where a man had died alone in bed, himself unaware that he carried the plague with him, waiting for the forgetful maid to bring him up his warm ale. Man still stopped into the Pied Bull Inn at least once a month; whether it was because it sometimes lay in his way or because of his recollection of the gruesome tale, he could not say. Much had been changed after the Fire, but many people could not help but remember the distinctive tragedies that had come to be associated with such places. How could the townspeople ever forget the helpless dying of over seventy thousand of their predecessors?

Man felt a sudden regret at not having borrowed some of Hoole's books. Had not the shutting-up of infected houses been expressly ordered by the Lord Mayor and the Aldermen in the summer of that year, before the worst ravages of August and September? The method had been brutal in its simplicity: the doors padlocked, the windows and doors with deal boards nailed across them, all entrance and exit forbidden by the two watchmen who between them carried out the watch and ward. Man's memory was faulty, but he thought there had been some precedents in the actons taken during the previous epidemic of 1603; but, this last time, the effects seemed to have been particularly harsh and, in the end, ironically disadvantageous. Wasn't it well over ten thousand dwellings at one point? And he had heard stories of certain shut-up people who had been murdered by their nurses or by the watchmen themselves, or they had been totally abandoned, or even purposefully starved to death.

His pipe had gone out long ago, but he kept it clenched tightly between his teeth. As he sat drifting back and forth between waking and sleeping, his thoughts began to assume a shape. It was — what? — fifty-seven years ago this month, Geoffrey Stannard would have been a young man, probably in his early twenties, the city dark with death, with the terror of invisible contagion, the few walkers shunning each other in silence, the houses marked with a long red cross in the middle of the door and the words 'Lord, have mercy upon us,' the alleys and lanes echoing with the clatter of the dead-cart and the bellman's monotonous 'Bring out your dead . . .'

'You were talking in your sleep.'

Man opened his eyes to find his wife bending over him, adjusting the blanket. The room was quiet in the grey half-light of late afternoon. He could hear faint rain and wind.

'What was I saying, then?'

Sarah motioned to him that the boy was asleep in their bedroom. She busied herself in the dark kitchen with getting ready his supper. Man's pipe lay in a fold of the lap-robe. His wife's voice came to him through the clattering of pots.

'You made, Sir, no more sense than you do when you are awake.'

He looked up at her mischievous tone, made as if to answer, and then thought better of it. This was one of the teasing assumptions which had grown up in their marriage: he was the one with all the great ideas, but it was she who had the store of common sense.

He pulled himself stiffly to his feet and draped the blanket carefully across the back of the chair. He struck himself smartly in the small of the back, where his cold seemed to have settled during his cramped sleep.

Before sitting down to the table, Man glanced into the bedroom. The boy lay curled beneath their best blanket in the heavy oak bed they had inherited from Man's father, sleeping the wholly instinctive sleep of the young, his hand cupped round his mouth as though he were dreaming of eating. Man wondered if he had fallen asleep at the table and if Sarah had had to carry him to bed.

But then, the child must weigh so little . . .

Vaguely troubled, Man settled himself before the table. Because he usually slept through dinner, his wife would make a comparatively larger supper: tonight, a veal pie with plums and sugar (Thursday was their day for meat), cheese, barley bread, and small beer. Man drained his first glass at one draught and lit the fresh pipe which he always liked to keep burning, to his wife's intense dissatisfaction, while he ate his meal.

At intervals, as they ate, he watched his wife across the table. He never ceased to marvel at her face which somehow managed to appear both yielding and strong. To Man, his wife seemed as elemental as a force of nature. Today, she looked larger, even more capacious, as if she could shelter and enrich the entire world.

They sipped their coffees and listened to the boy's steady breathing and to the sweeping of the rain.

'You talked, I think, something of Marseilles in your sleep.'

It was what had been preoccupying him most, as sleep had overtaken him. Man told his wife what he knew of the death of Geoffrey Stannard and of his conversation with Taylor Hoole. Sharing his work with her was important for both of them.

'But why Marseilles, husband?'

'You cannot be completely ignorant, Madam, of what special events have succeeded in setting half London astir these past two years. Marseilles, Arles, Toulon, and other cities of Provence—all visited by the plague. The name of Captain Chataud, whose ship is said to have brought the disease from Syria, has become a commonplace among the panicked citizens of London. Look you into any bookseller's or upon any stall—or into any of our own magazines which I am constantly trying to persuade you to read—and I believe you should find a host of dis-

cussions concerning the last plague and what due preparations should be begun for the next.'

'And are they so certain of its coming here?'

Man waved the smoke away from his face.

'Who can rightly say? The frenzy of the people has
somewhat abated of late—I mark its decline in the
streets—but the caution is yet in their minds and speech.
Rue and wormwood are taken into the hand, myrrh and
zedoary into the mouth. I have seen men walking abroad
with garlic and rue held in their mouths. And this
Tuesday last I passed a woman in Newgate Market who
was snuffing vinegar up her nose, sprinkling the same
upon her head-clothes, and holding a handkerchief
wetted with it to her lips. The people dread most what
they cannot see.'

His wife began to clear the table. Man saw that she was
frowning with worry.

'Do you make yourself anxious for a visitation, wife?'

'That is with God. I worry, Sir, that you may involve
yourself to your harm in this affair of last night.' She half-
turned towards the bedroom doorway. 'And what will
become of the boy? He is weak and homeless. If he were to
return to the streets and if the plague were there . . .'

Man heard in her voice a mingling of pleading and
demand.

'Must he leave with you?'

Man took the small cup of gin which she had poured
for him for his cold and moved slowly to the doorway.
The boy had rolled over in his sleep and now lay
diagonally across the bed, the blanket kicked off his bare
feet. Man stepped quietly into the room to fix the corner
over the thin legs. The boy was breathing harshly through
his mouth; and as the wind rattled in the window, he
shivered, though his skin felt warm.

As he came back through the doorway, Man finished

the last of his gin and reached for the greatcoat his wife held out to him.

'Where would I take him?'

At midnight, the Round House at the lower end of St Martin's Lane was almost as crowded and noisy as a market at noon. In the cellar could be heard the riotous singing of a pair of carefree drunkards and the muted weeping of a woman. On the ground-floor, a group of three aged watchmen was guarding a swagsman and discussing how the felon ought to be detained until morning. Their talk was good-natured, flavoured with the bitter-sweet smell of cheap gin in great wooden bowls. The prisoner seemed even more at ease than his captors, downing two bowls to every one of theirs. A stranger would not be able to distinguish readily, by appearance or behaviour, the offender from the officers of the law.

Above, in a cramped and smoky room, Man was sitting across a three-legged table from Constable Legge. Both were drinking gin from small, thick glasses. Two chairs stood apart from the table. In one, Taylor Hoole sat with his nervous hands crossed in his lap. The other chair had been taken by an unusually tiny and delicate man in his early thirties. He sat upright, balancing a dish of gin on his knee. Man could just see him over Constable Legge's left shoulder; and he thought that Edward Scripture had the kind of classic face which women always admire, but rarely love. The eyes, though weak and worried, missed nothing.

Gideon Legge was a stationary sort of man who seemed long settled in habits of self-assurance and self-indulgence. The size of his bloated stomach made his breathing sound laboured and incomplete. He was a constable of only middling talents, but one of the most prosperous geneva retailers in the parish.

He tipped a gourd-shaped bottle to refill his own glass

first, and then Man's, and handed it behind him to
Edward Scripture. After each taste, Legge smacked his
wet lips and exhaled with noisy relish.

'You're a bingo-boy after my own heart, Mr Man, and
there's no sin in it to my mind.'

Man drank far more slowly than the other. The gin
was of the cheapest and crudest kind, useful only to burn
thoughts of the cold dank night out of the mind.

'Often enough is it I've said 'tis men like you, Sir, that
keep the streets of London passable after darkfall.' He
spoke directly to Man, effectually ignoring the presence
of the other two. 'Many's the watch what don't care a
farthing for the law. We have us citizens now that can't
dare to step abroad come night, and I lay that to a
criminal failure of the watch and ward to secure the lanes
and alleyways of the town. Too many have misremem-
bered the promise of the Psalmist: "Thou shalt not be
afraid for the terror by night; nor for the arrow that flieth
by day; nor for the pestilence that walketh in darkness;
nor for the destruction that wasteth at noonday." Thus,
Sir, is your employment.'

He sat back and emptied his glass complacently.

'Is it your thought, then, that what we have here is an
actual visitation of the distemper?' Man had raised his
voice to make himself heard above the din of argument
that had begun to rise from beneath his feet. He wanted
also to speed the Constable's ambling conversation; the
watch had to be resumed in half an hour.

Constable Legge seemed taken aback, almost offended,
as if Man had presumptuously intruded into his own
private thoughts.

He hurriedly poured himself another drink. Man's glass
was still nearly full.

'What makes you say that, Sir, when I myself speak of
other matters? I suggest a civil drink among fellows to
arm us all against the night's chill, and you have now

twice brought us to a subject of which any of us as yet
know so little. And that, I might add, imperfectly.'

He reached into an inner pocket and brought out a
short, cracked pipe. While he busied himself with
lighting it, Man studied his face. He thought he could
almost mark the moment when the Constable regained
his stolid composure. A hard and proud man, he
reflected, but more than anything merely stubborn.

'Now that you have touched again upon last night, I
may say that the sheriff and the coroner have the
situation well in hand and intend to lay it before their
superiors tomorrow. Coroner Jessop sat this afternoon
at—or, rather, outside—the Stannard residence to
determine the circumstances and manner of death.'

'Were you yourself present, Sir?'

'I—ah—was not. I had other business elsewhere. But
Mr Petticrew—Mr Jessop's chief-assistant—and I have
something of an understanding betwixt us. He keeps me
as well informed of such matters as I keep him supplied
with this.' He lifted his glass. A look of curiosity and
mild disapproval passed into his face. 'And what, might I
ask, has brought you into this? Were you in any way
acquainted with the man Stannard? I know, Sir, that you
have been of some special help in the past in assisting
myself as well as certain of the bound-bailiffs in this city,
but those instances were in extraordinary times, were they
not?'

Edward Scripture was suddenly bent over by a fit of
coughing. Man could well remember the occasion when
Scripture's lungs had been badly scorched. Since then, he
had been constantly troubled by chest pains and rasping
breath. Man could locate Scripture in the darkest of
streets simply by his distinctive cough.

With a nod in the direction of Taylor Hoole, who was
sitting motionless as a stone statue, Man said:

'This gentleman here, who discovered Mr Stannard,

brought it to my attention. The scene affected him greatly as being in some ways unusual.' Man assumed an air of ingenuousness. 'My wife, you must know, is much given to following the popular fevers of the day. She is abed all the day with worry of a fresh epidemic abroad in the town. She has begged me to find the truth of the affair.'

Man could picture his wife's wry face, if she could have heard his description of her. He had, in fact, known no women — and very few men — as stalwart and forthright as she.

Constable Legge seemed appeased.

'You would do better, Sir, to keep such news from her, if the good lady is so easily troubled. Women, as we all know, cannot by nature possess the strength which sustains us men.

'I will tell you, then, what Coroner Jessop has concluded this day. I might add,' he went on, looking sternly at all three men in turn, 'that the conservators of this city do not wish to alarm the public without good reason. What is said here must remain here.'

He paused to underscore the official gravity of his words. To his listeners, he seemed a man who needed to be coaxed into telling something which he was already eager to tell.

'You have made mention, Sir, of the somewhat odd circumstances of Mr Stannard's death. Now, these very circumstances — argues Mr Jessop, and I think correctly — tell against the possibility of wilful murder. If a man were set upon a design to slay another, why then should he trouble himself with such elaborations? Why invite the curiosity of the passing crowd by shutting the man in by boarding up the doors and windows? There are surely many easier ways to go about his business. As Mr Jessop was heard to say, any murderer must have some reasoning behind his methods and behind his secondary actions, and here there can be none. Our first killer, Cain, slew his brother out of anger and made done with it. Murder is almost always quite simple.'

But, said Man to himself impatiently, murderers are not.

Constable Legge refilled his glass and slid the bottle to the centre of the table, no longer offering to pour some out for Man.

'On the other side of it, however, there is no doubt that the pestilence has raged these two years throughout France. And who can know that Mr Stannard did not travel there, perhaps during this past summer, when the heat and vapours of the sun spread the influence of the infectious effluvia? He may have carried back with him the doom of many. I myself, Sir, shall avoid that side of the street this coming month.'

'Had he the tokens upon him, do you know?'

'Mr Petticrew swears no. But which of us has not heard tales of the last plague, when sound men fell cold across their counters with flesh as clear as an untried girl's? Nay, these were said to be the most beyond hope, for the swellings upon the others often broke and began to cure. And many died of mere fright and surprise without any infection at all to notice or were frightened into idiotism and foolish distractions, despair and lunacy and melancholy madness. Never doubt, Sirs, that the distemper is the instrument which God uses to chastise the sinful. "The night cometh, when no man can work." Who can say what He may not accomplish in His own holy secrecy?'

Man could not decide whether Constable Legge's eyes shone more from fervour or from drink.

Taylor Hoole had finally moved his hands from his lap to clasp his head. He seemed far away.

'And something more. It is known that Mr Stannard had of late been reduced nearly to poverty. And I have read how those fearing worse reductions in 'sixty-five, to save the expenses, sometimes shut themselves in, or had it done to them; and, not having help available to them, died alone—almost, it might be said, by their own hands, if not by the hands of those employed to watch them.'

'Are you forgetting, Sir, that I found the man tightly bound and silenced? And if this were done by one of our own, either in his own interests or in that of the public, would he have not by now come forward? Most of us are honour-bound.'

Man was surprised at Taylor Hoole's sudden vehemence and at the disrespect implied in his words. Once again, Man wondered if his friend might not have a more personal interest in the case than he had yet revealed.

Constable Legge drew himself up and expanded his swollen belly to such an extent that the table was actually moved an inch nearer to Man.

"I, Sir, forget nothing. I spoke of such examples merely to indicate the desperate lengths the poor wretches were sometimes driven to. But, if we admit the probability of Mr Stannard's having been infected, may we not also consider that—distracted by the contagion—he may have himself arranged with another, possibly a dispassionate friend, to have himself shut up in this manner?'

'But why,' interrupted Man, 'in just such a fashion? Why so publish the nature of his own death? And why should any man willingly inflict upon himself the agonies of slow starvation?'

The Constable would not be put off his settled notions.

'I return, then, to my previous allusion. Perhaps some private person or some minor official like yourselves, having—as Mr Hoole has suggested—learned somehow of the man's dangerous condition, assumed the authority to enforce an isolation. Even here, the term "murder" would not apply. Remember that the new Quarantine Act, duly passed on the twenty-fifth of January last year, orders immediate death for anyone sick who attempts to leave an infected house or for anyone well who tries to leave after coming into contact with an inhabitant of such a dwelling. Anyone attempting to do so may be justly shot as one guilty of a felony.'

Taylor Hoole spoke up with bristling anger.

'And I could show you, Sir, an article from *Applebee's Journal* but four months later which describes with unspeakable horror the exact effect of such measures upon the people of Toulon, a city that lost two-thirds of its population.'

'Has not this Act been repealed?' asked Man in a quiet voice.

Flustered, Constable Legge bent over and knocked the bowl of his pipe against the leg of his chair. When he straightened up, his face was livid and hot.

'Jacobite treachery, Sir, plain and simple! Part of the late plot against our state. Besides, the principle remains. The man who arranged or helped to arrange Mr Stannard's death might well have done this city a service greater than any of us can know.'

The noise from the ground floor had quietened, but a dim murmur could still be heard from the cellar. In the room, the straining of Edward Scripture's suppressed cough blended with the soft creaking of Taylor Hoole's chair as he shifted about restlessly.

'And the candles taken from the night-cabinet to be burnt in the unused garret?'

'Could have been done by Mr Stannard himself, for whatever reason, long before his death. I will advise you that nothing has been taken from the house.'

'As well as we know.'

'And should we discover that anything seems wanting — well, Sir, there's many a simple cove in Drury Lane what would bite a darkened ken as soon as breathe.'

He had regained his confidence and appeared to

suppose the matter settled. He emptied his glass in one brusque movement and lifted himself slowly up from the chair. Swaying slightly on his feet, he looked at a point just above Man's head.

'I am sure you will agree with me that we do not wish to panic the people of this town, nor can we choose to ignore the unseen threat which even now may run amongst us. It is our work, gentlemen, to conserve the peace; and we all know the late economic chaos which is already plaguing so many of the people.'

With no consciousness of the irony of his choice of words, he strode uncertainly towards the door.

'We shall treat the unfortunate end of Mr Stannard as a signal warning to public security. Measures will be taken—but discreetly and on the official levels only, where more can be done and without inflaming the crowd. It is our duty to preserve the people from dangers from without and from within. Remember,' he concluded, his voice rumbling impressively, ' "For the thing which I greatly feared is come upon me, and that which I was afraid of is come unto me. I was not in safety, neither had I rest, neither was I quiet; yet trouble came." '

The three men were left sitting silent as shadows in the still room.

When he stepped out into St Martin's Lane, Man was startled to find a high clear sky and a brittle cold. The air stung his nostrils and made his head feel even more hard and throbbing. He bade goodnight to Hoole and Scripture and turned up the street.

The stocks, with the vertical whipping-post at their centre, stood stark as a spine before the Round House wall. Man could remember having watched it being built and the not unpleasant thrill of fear that he—as a young lad of thirteen—had felt at the prospect of the wrong-doers who would be punished there. That was three years before he had been first commanded into the *posse comitatus*, the beginnings of his work.

He passed by the area in which, during the day, work would be proceeding on St Martin's Church. The street was quiet, except at the lower end where a group of revellers was making for—he guessed—the overwhelming smells and sounds of the Bermudas district.

He continued up St Martin's Lane and turned off into Long Acre. The warmth and aroma of a night coffee-stall stopped him, and he stood for a few minutes, drinking a bitter cup and talking with the drowsy owner. The man could hardly be seen beneath a double muffling of cloaks, out of which his tired voice emerged in spurts of smoke.

When Man reached Drury Lane, he found the house directly before him. The face of it seemed inert and forbidding. It was an old, narrow house with lattice casement windows on the upper floors, now mostly crossed by wide boards. The house had recently been brought up to date by a covering of lath-and-plaster, and the ground floor had two newer sash-windows with wooden bars and small panes of glass. The entire building seemed to crouch—the front leaning back from the street, while the pointed roof-gables hung forward. The door was secured by a single piece of wood on to which had been tacked a sheet of parchment. Coming closer and showing the light of his lanthorn full upon it, Man could make out the signature of Coroner Jessop.

On the left of Stannard's house was another as old or even older; on the right, a chandler's shop belonging to one Sam. Caddick. Man could well imagine the confused collection of items within: bread, beer casks, hanging cheeses, sacks of coal, links, piled soap, pyramids of sand, bunches of candles. He knew such places well; a chandler's next to his father's house had been his own favourite haunt as a boy. Even now, Sarah used one in Old Street as oilman and grocer. And many mornings, if Hawkins's lay too far from his way home, Man would stop in at the nearest chandler's shop and join the market-women and street-sellers for breakfast, standing among them before the low counter and listening to their rough gossip.

Man stepped back into the middle of the street to look at the whole house. He wondered whom he could ask to let him see the inside. He wanted to roam about the rooms and read in them the character and the way of life of Geoffrey Stannard. But Man knew that, as a simple watchman, he had as little hope of seeing the house as he had of viewing the victim's body.

He looked up and down the deserted street. Here, he expected to meet at least a few prostitutes, but the cold was probably keeping them huddled into the narrower alleys. At the edge of his sight, he thought he saw a shadow slip between two buildings. It was not far off, but no sound of footsteps came to him through the darkness.

On the side opposite Stannard's stood a wider house with an apothecary's on the ground floor. Man noticed a mass of blacker shadow slumped over in the doorway. He walked across the street, gripping his watchman's staff more tightly in his right hand and lifting his light.

An old misshapen man lay curled asleep on the stones. He was shoeless and wore a tattered campaign coat that must have dated from the previous century. Man recognized him to be an abraham cove, a Poor Tom, one of a class of beggars who affected insanity to move compassion in passers-by. On his wind-worn face could be seen the marks of the pins he would insert during the day to make his pretence more frightening and convincing. He looked to be over sixty years of age, yet he could just as well have been forty-five.

The light, playing across his face, began to rouse him. Man crouched down and shook him gently by the shoulder. He could feel the sharp bone through the cloth.

The beggar's eyes flicked open, blurred with sleep and drink.

' 'Sbobs, a man might be let sleep of a night!'

He caught sight of Man's staff and lamp.

'The bube and ruffin take ye off, Darkm'n!'

He wrenched his coat farther up over his face and shrank back against the door. Man bent over into the stench of filth and disease.

'Will ye raise a cloud with me, friend?' As he spoke, Man set his lanthorn off to one side and took two pipes from his pocket. The beggar propped himself on to one elbow and watched Man stuff tobacco into the shallow pipe bowls. His eyes moved mistrustfully and his lips twitched.

They smoked for some minutes in silence, squatting together in the doorway out of the reach of the wind. A cripple hobbled up the street, muttering wordlessly to himself.

The beggar savoured the pipe slowly, rolling the smoke round in his mouth before sucking it to the bottom of his chest. He tried to put off exhaling as long as possible. This would most likely be his only pipe this month.

'Are you here long?' asked Man between puffs.

'Since the Union, p'raps.'

Man nodded towards the shut-up house across the way that stood as a block of shadow in the scarcely lighted street.

'Do you know the man of that place, then?'

'Stann'rd, is it? Saw him took out this day early.' He squinted his bleary eyes at Man.

'Is there talk on it in the street?'

'What I hear is what I hear. Bundled the cull in his own ken, some say, dead as Queen Anne the day after she died.'

'How long did he live here, do you know?'

The beggar spat sideways into a corner. He seemed to

grow more alert, making an effort to calculate the time.

'Twice it was. I see him this last two year, but he keeps himself to himself mostly, never comes out.'

'Who did for him, then?'

He pointed with the stem of the pipe in the direction of the chandler's shop.

'Caddick's girl runs it over. Fine country mort she is.'

'But he lived here before?'

'Was here when I come. Then he moves out in, say, 'eleven or so. Comes back monthly for the rent. Nice family there. The boy snucked me a drop when he could.'

The beggar appeared to think this an obvious hint, but Man chose to ignore it.

It was getting late and Man had to hurry. He reached into his pocket for a coin and passed it across to the beggar.

'How long has it been shut up?'

He massaged the coin between his fingers.

' 'Bout a month, I'd say. We hear one blue day he's gone off. Some business lay or other, we thought. Then a gent comes by in the lightmans and boards her up. Watched him at it I did, full on half a day.'

'What did he look like?'

The beggar did not seem to think the question important.

'Older gentleman he was. Somethin' poor and hungry like the most of us. Terrible thin and nervous. I ask for a bit off the son of a sow, but he's as close as Stann'rd himself.'

'Does he live in the area?'

'Don't know.' He sniffed and slipped the pipe into his shirt. 'Say, though, go'n ask him yourself, if you're so bothered to know.'

'And how would I find him?'

The beggar looked genuinely surprised.

'He finds you then, don't he? Or the beak. Or how's else

he to get what's his?'

Man felt suddenly as if he were hearing a strange language.

'What's your meaning, friend?'

'But he told me so himself, when I asks about the boarding. Name's Stann'rd. The son of the one what's died.'

A few minutes later, Man was walking down Drury Lane. He halted at the side of a small figure lying crumpled in the street. It was another boy, sleeping fitfully in a pool of rain. Man bent down and slipped a penny into the hand that was clenched about the thumb. Now the child could at least buy some breakfast.

It was a common practice of Man's, but tonight he did it out of habit, as though his thoughts were elsewhere.

CHAPTER 3

Hawkins would have to miss him this morning, thought Man, as he stood again in the middle of St Martin's Lane.

It was just after dawn. It was raining again, but in a drizzle that was so fine that it seemed no more than a cold silken sweeping against the face. The rain had kept on for three hours without slacking, and the churning of small rivulets could be heard from the rough kennel in the street.

Man's left shoulder hurt him, but it was now something more than a simple cold. It had happened in the night, as soon as he had come to Brewer Street from Drury Lane. He and two others had been called upon by an enraged citizen to rout a couple out of a low bawdy-house. The watchmen had gone in to the jeers of a dozen drunken, half-clothed men and women. In a room upstairs, they had found a dishevelled woman and a dark, starved-looking man, drinking gin and sprawled across two chairs. The scene had been loud and confusing. The couple had evidently been working what was called the cross-biting law upon the fat, smartly dressed man. The whore had enticed him to her room and accepted his money, only to be interrupted at the proper moment by her outraged 'husband'. But this victim had proved less docile than most, or more experienced. He now stood in the middle of the room, shouting curses at the woman and orders at the three watchmen. Man had been trying to talk to all of them at once, when the whore's bully had suddenly struck at him with a short knife. The point of the blade had passed through the folds of Man's greatcoat and into his shoulder before he could strike back with his staff. It took the other two watch ten minutes to subdue the screaming, scratching woman. They had come away with long red streaks running down their faces. By then, the victim had shifted his complaints from the scandalous behaviour of the poor to the inefficient enforcement of the parish watch.

Man flexed his stiff arm and wondered how encrusted with filth the knifeblade had been. He knew he was in for some special fussing from his wife for the next week or two. He had by now grown used to—and even rather fond of—Sarah's motherly panic.

He stepped carelessly across the street and headed for Tom's Coffee House. It was a badly kept place, with a brooding air of impending failure and poverty hanging over it like a pall. Man did not stop in here often now; but, as a boy, he could remember his father's doing a weekly business with the original owner, Thomas Nye, a man almost as round as one of his father's casks. Five years ago the business had been taken over by one named Digory Physick; and Man had never been able to bring himself to like the melancholy fellow, nor his masculine wife. It was she, in reality, who ran the House, with a lack

of success which belied the hardened heart she brought to
business affairs.

Digory Physick seemed not only surprised, but uneasy,
as he watched Man close the door behind him. It did not
bother Man; he was accustomed to the air of suspicion
with which most people greeted the watch. Man nodded
towards the owner and called for a cup. Soon, the warm
smell of brewing coffee began to circulate throughout the
empty room.

Man sat at the window, tamping the tobacco into his
pipe. He could hear someone, presumably Physick's wife,
moving about upstairs. The street was beginning to come
alive with people.

The owner brought a coffee to Man's table and
returned to the back of the room without a word. Man
thought him gloomy and preoccupied, but no more so
than usual. Digory Physick seemed always to be
contemplating the wasting death that would, in fact,
overtake him within the decade.

Man had to nurse two coffees for an hour and smoke
three full pipes before he saw Roger Petticrew come into
the shop. By that time, he had talked to a woman about
the bad season for vegetables, to a tailor about the falling-
off in the cloak trade, and had watched closely the
coming and going of a pair of rowdy young men, neither
of whom wore clothes that fitted him. As they left, Man
could hear Digory Physick damning all cloak-twitchers
under his breath.

Roger Petticrew was a man of stunted growth with the
closed and calculating manner of those who are
habitually ignored. He stepped quickly into the coffee
house and passed directly to the chair farthest from the
door, scowling as if he almost expected and hoped to find
his place occupied. As Man had been told, Roger Petticrew had been coming to this same shop every day for
over ten years.

Petticrew looked up from his news-sheet with annoyance, when Man set down his own coffee cup across from that belonging to the coroner's assistant. The two men seemed to take an immediate and inevitable dislike to each other: Man, to Petticrew's pasty smugness; Petticrew, to the watchman's grim and unalterable determination.

After the necessary introductions were completed, the atmosphere became, if anything, even more strained and unnatural.

'And your part, Sir, in this affair? I do not even speak here of authority, for you have none.'

Man took his own time in replying. He wanted to encourage Petticrew in his self-satisfaction.

'I am moved by concern for my good friend, Taylor Hoole. You know, of course, his rôle in this case, having talked with him yourself this time yesterday. What you cannot know, Sir, is how deeply Mr Hoole has been affected by his experience. I myself do not know why he should take on so, but that he does worries me not a little.'

Man did not much care to use his friend's personal turmoil as an excuse, but it was the only point of contact Man had in an affair with which he was in no way officially concerned.

Roger Petticrew sat back with a look of condescending distaste.

'Yes, Mr Hoole is another, I am afraid, who does not well know his proper place. His coming in here yesterday to interview me is an act for which he has not the least authority.' He assumed what he probably believed to be his most censorious attitude. His back straightened and his thin eyebrows drew together into a wrinkled arch. 'As for Hoole's questionable entry into the house in the beginning, I can assure you, Sir, that it will be closely examined at the proper time by those in a position to do so. And concerning your friend's morbid anxiety, perhaps it is due to the fact that he is the one who is most likely to have come into direct contact with the contagion. He did not strike me as a particularly fearless example of the parish watch.'

Man could feel his wrath rising against this puffed-up little man. If the conversation continued in this vein, he thought, it would soon be all he could do to keep himself from laying hands upon the insufferable official.

'The same would be true for Constable Legge who, I understand, made a preliminary inspection of the premises. Yet, when I spoke to him this last night, he gave no indication of any special fearfulness for his person. His concern was rather more general, more civic.'

And Man had been careful not to introduce the subject to the Constable; he had felt that he could learn more about the situation, and about the Constable himself, by merely letting him talk.

In the security of his favourite chair in his customary coffee house, Roger Petticrew allowed himself a small oily laugh.

'You can be certain, Sir, that Mr Legge's inspection of the house was fleeting at best. He is not one to expose himself lightly to any personal danger. After the body had been conveniently removed by some minor helpers, he most likely only opened the door quickly, looked in, and shut it again within the minute—all the while holding a gin-soaked handkerchief to his mouth. Such are the inspections customarily performed by Constable Legge. Of course,' he continued, toying with a corner of his news-sheet, 'in this instance, I cannot much fault him. Where the plague is concerned, even the strongest may weaken.'

'Are many, then, assured that the distemper is arrived?'

Roger Petticrew grew restive at this question, but Man could not decide whether it were due to the assistant's officious sensitivity or to a more private uncertainty.

Petticrew drew himself up, pretending to an authority which was beyond his dwarfish frame.

'The aim of our governmental bodies is to preserve civic peace, no matter what form of unrest may threaten. It may be that the reported negligence of the city officers during the last visitation, together with the alarming rumours from France, have made us more careful and meticulous to discover and contain any possible outbreak of the disease. And here the circumstances seem quite unmistakable, I should say.'

'On the surface, I grant it. Yet what if the death of Stannard should prove to be a more straightforward act of deliberate murder?'

Man again felt irked at having to suggest to so many people a possibility that had, from the first, seemed to him so obvious.

For once, Roger Petticrew appeared honestly surprised.

'Straightforward? I should hardly have called it that. Why would such an idea even present itself to you? I have known many murderers—no doubt, Sir, more than you— and I have never known one to resort to such arcane measures.'

This was evidently the time for an exact expression of Man's thoughts, the kind of task which he had always found the most difficult.

'The very methods to which you refer are those features which first caught my notice. That the plague should indeed have entered London and gone undetected by all, save by he who enforced starvation upon Mr Stannard, seems to me most unlikely. Why would this man be the only one to suspect Stannard's condition? What would make him assume sole responsibility for the shutting-up of the house? He must be among the most solicitous of Londoners to take this upon himself. And why has he not yet publicly accounted for his deed, if he feels he acted justly? He would be deemed a hero.'

Petticrew resumed his smug expression.

'Do not suppose, Sir, that these questions have gone unconsidered by our good Mr Jessop, one of the most able coroners in this city. He has wisely concluded that the person or persons who participated in the death of Mr Stannard were and are yet motivated by the best desires not to add to the already inflamed fancies of the people. These are chaotic times, Sir. My own cousin has this month removed himself with his family into the country. Your friend, Mr Hoole, could better inform you of the extent of the unease within the city. I understand from my conversation with him that he is especially well-read in the subject—perhaps, may I say, too much so. As for your suggestions of a private malice, I find that I must agree with Mr Jessop that such an interpretation of the facts would be most unreasonable.'

As Man had expected, Roger Petticrew—like Constable Legge—could do nothing more than echo the opinions of his superiors. The only advantage Man had in talking to Petticrew was that it brought him one step nearer to the sources of information in the parish offices. And this would be as close as he could come.

It would be useless for Man to try to explain his own understanding of the case. To him, too, the circumstances of the act seemed complicated, but no more irrational than some other murders he had witnessed. The killer might well have reasoned that a pretence of the plague would help to avert suspicion, as it had succeeded in doing. Or there might be some darker purpose.

Here, for Man to formulate his thoughts would call for an eloquence which he knew he did not possess. How could he speak of the many whom he had known who lay awake all night, reliving imagined injuries, unable to escape from the face which hatred had made dear, the life that by its mere existence blighted their own? How could he describe to such a one as Roger Petticrew the anger that grows beyond its cause or the bitterness that intrudes into every thought? Or the emptiness that justifies any outrage?

They were now surrounded by a roomful of shopkeepers and vendors, drinking and talking or simply trying to strengthen themselves for another day. Which of these, reflected Man, might tomorrow be driven by fear or pain to an act of violence? To how many had it already happened—who now felt, by reason of their momentary brutality, different and apart?

Man felt a sudden urge to shock the man across from him, to watch that smart face pale in disbelief.

Petticrew drank off the last of his coffee and began to arrange his coat about his frail body, supposing the conversation had come to an end. Mrs Digory Physick—a bloated woman with swollen breasts that rocked across her belly—took his money and his cup. The coroner's assistant nodded at Man with a grunt and was in the act of rising from his chair, when Man said as casually as he could:

'And, naturally, Mr Jessop must feel even more sure of his stand, knowing that the man who shut up Stannard in his house was his own son.'

Man emerged into a street where the air was crisp and damp, but teeming with a growing crowd of people and horses and carts.

The first person to cross in front of him was a barker who was crying: 'Cloaks, coats or gowns, what d'ye lack, Sir?' The vapour of his breath trailed behind him over his shoulder like a scarf, and the harshness of his voice lingered between the high walls bordering the street.

Man turned right, up St Martin's Lane. He wanted time to think, and he did not at all dread the prospect of the long walk home. He planned to make for High Holborn and the King's Way, bearing eastward. It would be colder so close to the open fields, but he relished the view of the country.

He had expected, of course, that Coroner Jessop felt completely certain that Geoffrey Stannard had lived and died alone, without family or heirs. Man himself had little doubt of it. The parish records were accurate enough. There was always the possibility of an illegitimate son, but a bastard does not usually announce himself as such to every passing beggar. There was, too, the odd chance that Stannard might have had a son and, for some reason, refused to acknowledge him. And the records of that birth might have been among those lost in the Great Fire. Petticrew had finally stated Stannard's age to be eighty; the beggar had said the 'son' was an 'older gentleman'—perhaps in his sixties. So, in 1665, the one would have been twenty-three and the other a boy of five or so.

But Man did not really believe that the murderer—if the man who had boarded up the house was, in fact, the same who had killed Stannard and not some second party—was truly related to the victim. Sons do sometimes, incredible as it seemed to Man, kill their fathers, but rarely with such fine forethought and care. So the man who spoke to the beggar in Drury Lane must have been lying; yet why should he decide to choose such a flagrant and distinctive lie? He would have known that the truth could be easily found out. Even the beggar himself might well have known better.

Although Man, with his long experience with human inventiveness, did not for an instant cease to regard the death as anything less than homicidal, the parallels with the Great Death of fifty-seven years ago and with the current mania were still too significant to be discounted. There must be some connection, and some hidden reasoning behind that connection, that must be understood. Even should the murderer himself be never apprehended, Man would continue to feel the need to understand.

In High Holborn he was assailed by the racket of long-distance coaches and waggons speeding towards Newbury and Exeter, Bristol and Swindon. Droves of pigs and sheep forced him into doorways. An oyster-seller bumped his cart against Man's shin.

The vendor must have wondered at the fleeting smile which passed across Man's face. Man was thinking of his talk with Roger Petticrew. Although he had quickly and peevishly dismissed the possibility of Stannard's having had a son, the coroner's assistant had been put back into his chair by Man's abrupt statement. And, after a short time, the watchman had come to realize that Petticrew was exactly the kind of man he had guessed him to be: the kind who, given the right amount of coaxing and flattery, would become as gossipy as an old washerwoman at the riverside. Man had had to sift through a great deal of petulant bickering and conceited opinions to get at some useful information, but eventually he had come away from Tom's Coffee House with as much as he needed.

The facts were few, but important. They had to do mainly with the various changes in Stannard's financial fortunes over the years, fluctuations which were only a small personal part of those taking place in the city at large. As Petticrew had mentioned before, the current panic was not due solely to a renewed dread of the plague, but also to an economic mania which was in many ways even more insidious and unsettling.

Geoffrey Stannard had been born in 1642 in a house in Drury Lane, not far from the one in which he was to die. His father was a merchant trading in textiles whose poor sense of management never succeeded in raising the family out of poverty. When the son grew to manhood he came to prefer speculation to retailing as a more dramatic means of making his fortune. In 1665, Geoffrey Stannard was still living in the family house in Drury Lane, although he had begun to act as a jobber and broker in the City. The bare outline of his career suggested a slow and imperfect rise to a moderate prosperity, culminating in a modest windfall with the wave of speculation at the founding of the Bank of England in 1694. He had suffered, four years later, the common fate of all brokers, when they were evicted from the Royal Exchange; but, by the turn of the century, he had managed to secure his middling position in the financial world. By then, he had been living for over thirty years in the Drury Lane house outside of which Man had stood the night before.

Man came upon a family of beggars huddled in the road. They were all there: father, mother, young ones, a baby wrapped in a rat-eaten shawl. On the stones beside them lay a crude sign detailing the history of their misfortunes. Their clothes were indescribably ragged, and even the faces of the children looked blank and confused. Man paused to drop some coins into the empty basket and passed on.

The lowest forms of destitution, thought Man, usually engender a sort of brute endurance for the life of few prospects. But for those like that beggar family—who, if the story on their sign was to be believed, had fallen through no fault of their own—poverty must be an especially bitter fate. Geoffrey Stannard must have been born into such a home, where ambitious dreams of sudden wealth are never allowed to die and constant fears of disaster spur a man on to any attempt. They who are used always to expect more will come to demand more.

So, in his sixty-ninth year, Geoffrey Stannard saw still another chance to realize his greatest hopes. He became one of the many speculators who followed Robert Harley in the founding of the South Sea Company.

Something nudged against Man's boot, and he looked down to find a hard wooden ball between his feet. He picked it up and gave it back to the little girl who had come running anxiously across the street towards him. She looked up at him with a grave face, as if the two of them were exchanging great confidences.

Man reviewed his memories of those days. Excitement ran high over ornate visions of lucrative trade with Spanish America. Of course, said everybody, the War of the Spanish Succession will soon end; and then the trading of slaves will be opened to the immense profit of all. South America and the Pacific were ripe for unbridled commerce. Fortunes might be made in a day.

Holders of Navy and Ordnance bonds were offered stock with a guaranteed interest of six per cent. Man had himself considered buying in on a smaller scale, only to be dissuaded by the cautions of his wife. He was not one to be readily allured by promises of quick and easy riches, but the opportunity had seemed so particularly inviting and safe. They had talked it over for a week, often angrily, before Man gave in.

When the Treaty of Utrecht was made two years later, Man began silently to bless his wife's foresight. The imposition of an annual tax on imported slaves and the restriction against the Company to send only one ship each year, which could not even enter the Pacific, began to deflate the dreams of speculators. Man could imagine the disappointment Geoffrey Stannard must have felt at the news. Petticrew had hinted that Stannard must have over-extended himself dangerously in his commitment to the Company. The modest success of the first voyage in 1717 fell alarmingly short of everybody's expectations. It was at this time that Sarah Man, good woman though she was, indulged herself in a little well-earned pride at the expense of her mollified husband.

As he turned into the relatively deserted King's Way,

he wondered how seriously Stannard had panicked at the waning of his hopes. Man saw him as one in whom a desperate drive for gain lay in a delicate balance with a dogged tenacity in the face of disillusionment. He guessed that he was the kind of man who would every day be fired with some new scheme which, if or when it failed in its promise, would occasion a fresh inspiration to try something even greater. Stannard's character must have been one that was not so much unquenchable as simply indefatigable.

Still, Man silently reminded himself, whatever the temporary setbacks, the postwar boom had given many continuing cause for hope. The accompanying excitement in France over the Mississippi Company seemed to offer an encouraging example. When King George I became governor of the Company in 1718, public confidence in the enterprise surged ahead, and the Company was soon paying 100 per cent interest.

But it was the year 1720 which saw the most delirious boom in South Sea stock. When the Company proposed to take over nearly the whole of the national debt, Man had seen staid brokers in 'Change Alley slapping each other boisterously on the back. Perhaps the fever had even persuaded Stannard to buy further into some of those other ventures, less genuine and more hazardous, that were being offered by the hundreds of swindling promoters infesting the Alley.

Man stopped in front of the Red Lion cockpit, Gray's Inn, and admired the view of its pointed roof against the backdrop of the bowling green, faded in the saturated air. He could recall coming here as a young man of one-and-twenty to see the great week-long cockfighting programme between the birds of Westminster and those of the City. Four guineas a battle and a hundred guineas the odd battle! That was in his bachelor days; a few years later he was settled down with Sarah. She did not care for the raw noise of the cockpit.

He sat down on a post to rest. From an inside pocket, he took out the scrap of paper on which he had noted a list of figures from Roger Petticrew's clerkly memory. Why had Man even bothered to write them down? Probably because they gave him a bare outline of the events which had occurred in a part of society with which he personally was not very familiar. In January 1720, South Sea Company stock had stood at 128½; 330 in March; 550 in May; 890 in June; 1000 in July and August. Then, the bubble had burst. In September—two years ago this month—it dropped to 175 and in December to 124. Even Bank of England stock had fallen from 263 to 145.

Man could read in these numbers the cold facts of the city-wide chaos he remembered so vividly. Respectable gentlemen fleeing abroad, not a few of them throwing themselves from high windows. The following February he had studied in the journals the report of the House of Commons investigation. The scandal had involved the highest levels of society: Aislabie expelled and imprisoned, the Earl of Sunderland and Charles Stanhope only narrowly acquitted, the estates of the Company's directors confiscated. Only the Great Man Walpole and his ministry had emerged unscathed.

How had Geoffrey Stannard weathered the storm, the total collapse of his greatest dream? The most immediate effect, Man now knew, was to return Stannard to the house in Drury Lane at the end of September, 1720. It must have been the most bitter of disappointments to him. He had managed to escape from the squalor of Drury Lane nine years before, take up new residence in the more fashionable area on the west side of Bedford Row, and rent out the old house to a carman and his family. To have to descend again, at the advanced age of seventy-eight, into the meanness he thought he had left forever behind him, must have seemed to Stannard something of a preliminary death. He would try anything to set himself free once more.

Man looked up sharply, stiffened with surprise. He had suddenly realized how near he must be at this moment to Stannard's other house, the one in Bedford Row, which now stretched southward almost directly before him. He glanced up at the leaden sky and figured the time to be close to eleven. He thought he might have just enough time for a quick look before continuing homeward for lunch and a nap. Sarah would understand. And, besides, she was most likely still busy with the boy.

As he entered Bedford Row, a commotion at the side of the road brought him to a halt. It was not a violent outbreak, but all the more noticeable in a neighbourhood that was otherwise so still.

Not far off from where he stood, a burly man of about fifty dressed in a thick coat that suggested the sea was bending over a common street-child, sprawled helplessly on the frozen ground. Man could not tell from the tone of the voice whether he were scolding the child, as so many worthy citizens felt themselves obliged to do, or whether he were merely expressing his anger on the child's behalf. As Man approached, he saw the seaman make as if to lay hands upon the child.

It was perhaps because of the boy who even now was being sheltered within his own home that Man spoke up more forcefully than was usual with him.

'Hold off, Sir! I would have you offer no harm to this poor boy!'

The seaman turned with a start, as if he had heard but not understood. Man was shocked to see a rough hard face in which he could note both wrath and sorrow.

Pointing down at the bewildered boy, he grumbled at Man:

'Are you, Sir, responsible for this unfortunate? I warn you, you will have much to answer for, if you are.'

The two stood facing each other. Man was the shorter by a few inches, and he had to look up slightly to meet the other's eyes. He could not match the seaman's wide shoulders and massive chest, but he confronted him without flinching.

As Man looked into his eyes — surrounded by the strained leathery skin of the adventurer, but surprisingly gentle — he began to understand that the two of them might have the child's welfare in common.

Man dipped his head a fraction and softened his tone.

'Forgive me, Sir, if I have mistaken your intentions; but I have seen so many abuse these luckless orphans of the streets that I naturally thought the worst. I perceive now that your concern for this boy is as honest and Christian as my own.'

There was something almost comical about the scene: the two strong men standing over an unwashed and emaciated boy of five or six, now totally confused and for the moment almost forgotten. The air gradually filled with a stinging mist.

The outline of the seaman's solid body relaxed.

'I should expect that any man, be he Christian or pagan, could not help but be moved by London's most deplorable disgrace. My business, Sir, takes me often through the streets of this city; and I have found no sight so shameful as this inhuman scattering of abandoned children, some of them dead and many of them dying. I wonder that the governors of these parishes do not feel it their duty — as mere men, if not as public officials — to take these sad children up. I have seen more common decency among those who are called savages.'

Man could make no answer. The two men then turned to questioning the boy. The child seemed sincerely astounded at the concern of the two strangers. After learning that he lived with a group of beggars in the cellar of a nearby alehouse, the men each gave him a coin and told him to take himself off for something to eat. Together, they watched him as he ran awkwardly across the road and out of sight.

The seaman shook his head.

'There's not much we can do for him now, I fear. And this is but one of thousands.'

A quarter of an hour later, the two men were seated at a table near a crackling fire in a minuscule tavern in Portpool Lane. Between them, on the splintered table, lay steaming dishes of broth and potatoes. Each held a cup of hot tea.

Man took to his companion at once. Captain Thomas Coram had spent most of his life alternating between sea travels and the promotion of philanthropic designs. Originally from Dorset, he was settled in Massachusetts in the 'nineties. A learned man as well as a working shipwright, he was a vocal champion of the Church, public education, and the needy. Three years ago, when sailing for Hamburg in the *Sea Flower*, he had been stranded off Cuxhaven and forced to witness the plundering of his vessel by the native population. Now living in Rotherhithe and doing business in the City, he impressed Man as a gentleman of deep convictions and a restless urge to do whatever needed to be done.

Their talk centred on the London poor, especially those innumerable children left to beg or starve in the streets by hopeless, drunken or criminal parents. Coram could hardly check his rage, as he described the miseries he had daily seen on his walks through the streets. He swore that he had been a personal witness to the shocking spectacle of innocent children who had been murdered and thrown aside on to dunghills.

'Think you, then,' he spoke around a mouthful, 'as so many do, that all of this can be laid to the present rabid consumption of spirits? Not I, Sir. There is more behind it than that. There is the black carelessness in the hearts of the people. How are we to cure them of that?'

When Man suggested that, with the proper planning and subscriptions, a man of his energy and vision might someday be able to establish some kind of hospital for such foundlings and strays, Coram sat silent, slowly chewing his food and considering.

'Aye, a long work, that.'

Man himself thought of his tender-hearted wife and of the boy. What was to be done, now, with Toby?

With no particular motive in mind, Man asked about Coram's father. After a few general family reminiscences, Coram mentioned at random that his father had been captain of a ship which had gained great repute during the year of the Great Plague as a floating haven for those who wished to flee from the encroaching infection. Coram himself had not yet been born, but he could remember hearing from his mother and uncle of the selfless courage of his father. Man sat listening pensively to the story: of the ships, each crowded with three or more families, lying in rows in the breadth of the river, extending from Ratcliff and Redriff down as far as the head of Long Reach—perhaps several hundreds of sail, more than ten thousand people sheltered from the violence of the contagion.

Had his family, by any chance, known any from the neighbourhood of Drury Lane?

Possibly, but he could not now recall any names. He had only heard the kind of tales which all families hand down among themselves, and it was all so long ago. Of course, as everyone knew, the plague's first victim had died in that street.

So long ago . . . This was what perplexed Man the most. If Geoffrey Stannard's death were in some strange way related to the Great Plague, what was it that could reach across a span of fifty-seven years? What kind of fear or hatred could last that long?

The two men separated in the street, Coram promising to call on Man soon. Man watched him walk off towards the City, the seaman's head constantly turning from side to side as if on watch, his body swaying with the lumbering grace of the mariner.

A weak sun had broken through the overcast sky, but the air felt even frostier than before.

Man was tired, with an ache deep in his bones. He did not think he had the strength to work his way back to Bedford Row for a look at Stannard's house. It would have to wait.

He turned up Gray's Inn Lane, wondering why he should suddenly notice the smell of winter in the wind.

CHAPTER 4

The first thing every customer noticed upon entering the shop was the absence of light. Not only were the windows small and filmed over with a hardened layer of grease, but the main room was so cluttered with merchandise that whatever daylight managed to filter through the half-closed door seemed quickly to become absorbed by the stacks of dusty boxes and the shelves of disorganized stock. It was the kind of place in which it was impossible to walk without having to step over or around something.

A musty smell of meats and cheeses, oil and tallow thickened the air. The stale reek of gin overpowered all other odours. Nothing smelled fresh or new.

At almost any hour of the day or night the shop was crowded with the shrill voices of noisy women and bickering children. Nobody left without first drinking a cup of gin, and mothers could be seen handing down the last few drops to their children, seated cross-legged on the broken floor.

Nothing was wanting: discoloured barrels sprawled among the dull glow of used bottles; soiled linen lay draped across sacks of sand; pyramids of bitter-smelling coal stood loosely piled in corners; cracked kitchen utensils hung from twisted hooks; opaque glasses were jammed into crusted pots, which were set into buckets with sprung bottoms and warped sides. The room looked like a self-contained world in which anything imaginable might be found.

Every Saturday afternoon Nancy Flanner would welcome the opportunity to escape for a moment from the jumbled world of the chandler's shop and slowly cross the street to the apothecary's to buy Samuel Caddick's weekly supply of 'mixture'. Her employer suffered from epileptic seizures and a wife whose ambitions reached beyond the dark walls of the shop and the confining poverty of Drury Lane. After a few minutes' chatting with the druggist's apprentice, Nancy would reluctantly return to the shop and to her place behind the low counter. She liked the fair-haired apprentice: he knew about books and talked fine.

This Saturday afternoon, as she re-entered the chandler's, she noticed a man who must have come in while she was out. She saw a middle-aged man of solid build, a bit above average in height, with sloping shoulders, a compact chest, and long angular arms. The forehead was high and ridged, and the nose was sharp; but the mouth had a delicacy that was almost feminine.

The most extraordinary feature of the man were his eyes: wide and staring and clear. He seemed to see everything at once, both singly and as a part of the whole.

Nancy recognized him by his greatcoat as one of the watch and ward, although he now carried neither staff nor lanthorn. She had never seen him in the shop or in the street before.

She came up to him, as he was inspecting a pile of old journals.

'Something I can help you to, Sir?'

He turned to her and spoke in an even, serious voice.

'I am told that you, Miss, were perhaps as well acquainted with Mr Geoffrey Stannard as any.'

Nancy Flanner nodded quickly twice. She looked to be a girl completely without guile, wanting only to be able to keep herself ready to serve others.

'And I still can't believe he's gone from us, the poor gentleman. I mean to say, we all of us thought he'd been off on business somewhere this past month. And then of a sudden them parish officers come on the Thursday and carry him away. 'Course, he was well on in years and all, and not at all a strong man.'

Her eyes faltered, and she reached out needlessly to straighten the stack of yellowed journals.

'There's talk that he went of some disease or other. Some are saying 'tis the plague again. Else why would he have had to be shut up in his own house like that? It fair gives me the chills, it does, to think of him lying there upstairs all alone with no one to do for him and no one to know. It must have been right awful for him, him knowing that he couldn't get out and all.'

The man looked at her so keenly that she moved nervously off towards the boxes of stationery. A fat market-woman dressed in a man's coat came into the shop, bringing a mass of cold in with her. Out of a door hidden somewhere in the back wall stepped Caddick's wife—a sharp, wiry woman with permanent wrinkles etched from chin to mouth—who glanced with impatience at Nancy Flanner and at the quiet man in the greatcoat.

'But did none of the neighbours hear anything? Surely a man would not lie quietly dying for an entire month without making some effort at signing for help.'

'Why, the poor soul was, I'm sure, so weak and

unminded that he could not bring himself to the windows.'

'And if, indeed, Mr Stannard had been afflicted with the distemper and forced to allow himself to be confined, he would yet require food and drink to be brought in from the outside. It was you, was it not, who daily provided for him?'

'It was, Sir, since my father broke his leg on the wharves and died from it. My mother still takes in needle-work down in Wapping; but there are five of us children, and I am the oldest, so I had to take what work I could find. I send her some little money every month, Sir, all I can spare. 'Tis a hard life for us.'

She spoke with the simplistic pride of those who only do what is expected of them.

'Bread and coffee of the morning, soup and ale for the afternoon and night. Mr Stannard did not want for much.'

'Did he, then, pay Mr Caddick regularly?'

She showed the confidential discomfort of the dependable servant.

'Well, I fear that since the late troubles in the City, he had been something hard put to it. It gave Mr Caddick no end of worry.' She lowered her voice. 'Or Mrs Caddick, rather.'

'And this past month? How were you informed that Mr Stannard would not be needing anything?'

'Why, I don't know. 'Twas Mr Caddick said to me, and I just thought as it was Mr Stannard himself as told him.'

A few more customers entered from the street, carrying a smell of dampness in the folds of their coats. The man looked over Nancy Flanner's shoulder in the direction of the harried Mrs Caddick. He leaned forward and spoke apologetically.

'Pardon me, but I don't mean to take you from your work. If you think it might be better, I should like to look round the shop and speak more to you — if you do not object, of course — during those times when you are least busy.'

And with that he wandered off in a distracted manner to browse among the baskets of bread. He seemed to take an odd delight in the wild assortment of sights and smells which filled the chandler's shop. He even stopped to finger some cheap three-cornered hats of dark felt and to stir a delta of loose coals with his toe. The shop absorbed all his attention; he evidently felt no self-consciousness at either the vexed stares of Mrs Caddick or the uneasy curiosity of Nancy Flanner.

She moved uncertainly towards the back of the room and submitted herself to the bitter upbraidings and snide accusations of her employer. Did Miss believe that she was being paid to dawdle her time away with a single customer? Was this still another beau, and was he not a bit too advanced in years for her? Not that that had ever stopped her before . . .

For the next hour, the conversation between Nancy Flanner and the persistent man in the greatcoat developed piecemeal during lulls in business and during the repeated absences of Mrs Caddick, as she hurried upstairs to attend to her husband who was today bedridden with an especially bad attack.

Gradually, Nancy Flanner lost any sense of her being formally interrogated by the unknown man. It was rather as if he were merely inviting himself to share her confidences. Even his most direct questions came to seem little more than the casual chat between a young girl and her visiting uncle.

Had she got to know Mr Stannard at all well?

Oh, very well indeed! He was a most fine gentleman, he was, quiet and reserved in his old age, but with a good deal of spirit and intelligence left in him.

Did she use only to deliver his daily supplies to him and

go, or did she perhaps stay over for a minute or two for a talk?

Here a small girl interrupted them with a written order from her ailing mother.

What was it, then? Well, yes, she would stop now and again for a small taste, and of course Mother Caddick would scold her roundly for it when she finally did get back. Even at his age, Mr Stannard had a preference for a royal bob of the afternoon.

And he had such stories to tell! He had seen and done much in his years. She had always had a fascination for those times of the last century—she being a storm-child herself, having been born in 1703, the year of the Great Storm—and he had been able to tell her such things of those days as she could not even think to dream of. Oh, and he said he had been one of those who had helped to contain the Great Fire in the City and had won great praise for his works.

The Year of the Great Plague? No, she could not recall that he had mentioned anything of that. Strange, that, that he should speak so little of it and then to die that way . . .

At this point she scurried off to thank a shabbily dressed man as he was leaving the shop with a bottle. She stood for a while at the door, bidding him farewell, seeming to be longer at it than was necessary.

When she got back, she stopped and looked round her in confusion. Now where had he gone to? The half-dozen people moving aimlessly about the shop were all women. Two were being helped by Mrs Caddick to dishes of gin; the rest were taking their time shopping, enjoying the close warmth of the room.

Could he have somehow got upstairs, with or without Mrs Caddick's permission, to talk to the invalid shopkeeper? What would Mr Caddick tell him? Nancy Flanner had always known that neither one of her employers much liked her; but the chandler himself had lately turned particularly cold towards her, even after all those mornings upstairs with his wife away at the market. It was something which she had never been able to understand.

Suddenly the man in the greatcoat rose from behind a row of casks with a kitten in his arms. The animal often got into the shop, to the petty annoyance of Mrs Caddick. Now, the man was stroking it as tenderly as if it were a lost child.

He wanted to know if Mr Stannard had ever revealed to her much about his personal life.

She knew he had never been married, of course. He had always seemed to her to be the kind of man who would prefer to live out his life alone, without the bothersome company of any other person.

No, the very idea! A son? Mr Stannard had simply not been that sort of man. He had always been far too busy taking care of his financial affairs to encumber himself with any legal or natural family ties. Not that he was not a man of surprisingly great reserves of personal energy . . .

The kitten jumped out of the man's arms and bounded out into the pale sunlight.

Her father had had a friend who had lived well into his eighties, but so crippled and melancholy with the gout those last twenty or thirty years. Mr Stannard, now, had been one of inexhaustible determination. Forever in a hurry to try something new. His mind, too, had remained unusually sharp and inventive. No, he was in no way confined to bed or house; she thought he stayed within doors by his own choice, owing to his reduced circumstances. He was a proud man, never pitiful or idle.

Nancy Flanner appeared eager to convince her listener of the truth of what she said. By frequent glances towards the ceiling, she seemed to be implying that her employer would do well to imitate such a man as Geoffrey Stannard.

Her eyes involuntarily rested on the pile of old journals and cheap books. The watchman followed her gaze and frowned.

Abruptly, as if she had just now come to understand the relevance of it, she added that Mr Stannard had shown an excessively nervous dread of death. She remembered he had been talking once of an acquaintance of his in the City who had killed himself in despair at the recent loss of his fortune on the Exchange. Even to be thus close to death had totally unnerved him. He had, she said with some disgust, almost whimpered aloud in speaking of his own approaching end. If only it could somehow be avoided or delayed!

Yes, of course, but there was something more. Mr Stannard made himself most frantic at the thought of his dying in poverty, the ignoble and agonizing death that so often comes with squalor and disease. It seemed sometimes that he was ready to do anything, to anyone, to preserve himself from an early or painful death. But, then, he had never been a religious man, so he was left without those consolations which most folk enjoy.

Nancy Flanner could, at times, be a smug and superstitious young girl. By the time she had returned towards the front of the shop from still another tense conference with Mrs Caddick, she had smartly concluded that all Mr Stannard's manic fears had been but his presentiment of the falling of the distemper upon him. Perhaps he had learned that one of his friends or associates might have passed the infection to him. Perhaps he himself had discovered the tokens upon his person. Now that she thought of it, he had of late seemed so easily excitable and overwrought.

The watchman turned from Nancy Flanner to rummage casually among the merchandise. His last questions came quickly, as if he had now lost any interest in the subject.

No, she had never had any occasion to visit the unused garret of the house next door.

Well, on the very day that the house had been shut up, she had been called to attend to her poor mother, stricken with a sudden fever.

Oh yes, she had sorely missed the old gent this past month. And him going off without even saying goodbye! No, she didn't mean it quite like that. But she thought she could recall someone telling her that he had been called to some business or other up north somewhere.

As if from nowhere, a spindly form appeared between the watchman and the girl and spoke in a low, strained voice.

'Beggin' your pardon, I'm sure, Sir, but Miss Nancy here has got to go to market for us. Nancy, get you off and be quick about it. You know what we need.'

Flustered, Nancy Flanner moved hesitatingly towards the door, thanking the gentleman and hoping she had been able to be of some help to him.

The last she saw of the man in the greatcoat was a glimpse of his straight back passing behind the thin figure of Mrs Caddick into the rear of the shop.

And as he made his way, without a word of explanation, towards the staircase leading to the upper floors, George Man was asking himself what exactly he had managed to learn from that most serviceable young woman.

'If you were to ask me, Sir, I'd say that Mistress Nancy would do better to be more mindful of her proper place. I never saw one to give herself such airs so. You would do well, Sir, to apply to me for what you wish to know, and give small thought to what that girl says.'

'Is she, then, so little to be trusted?'

'She has her uses, I'll not deny it. As you can see, I am far from being a sound man. I suffer from a host of illnesses, each one of which separately could well prove fatal. We enjoy an active trading in this shop — have done for these twenty year — too much for Mrs Caddick to manage alone. We've had upwards of a score of girls, but none of them stay on for long. Can't depend on any of them these times. And Nancy, I'll say here between us gentlemen, is somewhat worse than most of her kind. In and out all the time, and more gabbling than working.'

'Yet she is here long, and you yet keep her on.'

'Out of condescension towards her mother, who my wife has known since girlhood. The father had ne'er a face but his own. He's well out of it.'

'She seems to have got on well enough with Mr Stannard.'

'As well, Sir, as any Nanny gets on with any man in any of your common trugging-kens in Drury Lane! She would most likely oblige you, too, for the asking. And your Mr Stannard was another one — as ancient and poxed a meat-monger as ever I've seen! One's never enough for the likes of the both of them. It's them what never seem it do it most.'

'You were acquainted with Mr Stannard, then, for precisely how long?'

'He was here when I come — year of Queen Anne. 'Course, he got too good for us later on — do you know of him and the South Sea Company? — and he let the house out to the Parfrey family and settled on to higher ground. Nice family that was, clean and respectable, but ill-fortuned. Then back he comes, well-whipped. Did my heart good to see him have to dismount the great horse and lower himself down into the Lane again. Then he don't come out much, too proud to be proud. He gives us his business then. Too rat-poor to go further afield. And Nancy's pleased enough to do the service lay for him.'

'Do you mean she was over there somewhat more than she needed?'

'Well, Sir, all I will say to that is that she's to bed upstairs here, yet often enough is it I've heard her comings and goings in the dark night. A man on his back gets to notice these things. Thank God, when they took him off t'other day, they finally put an end to such shameful night-work. And him said to be gone and all.'

'You say the man was not well-known in the street. But was he, among those who did know him, well-liked?'

'Hard cider goes down smoother. A man what lives only for himself has no time for the rest of us. Stannard'd not so much as pass the time o'day with you. Him with his secret schemes to see a new pile! Always rumouring it about about some new idea or other that'd set him up again. Not that any of us ever saw the head on it. Might as well put a blind man to wash a Negro. What'd he need for at his age? He lived as comfortable as any of us. And him with no one to leave it to when he does kick. But he was always the same, even before he left to come back.'

'Have you yourself ever been to the house?'

'Have you eyes, Sir? Am I not without legs here? Not that I didn't carry myself over there once or twice to try the old pinch-gut for his bill, for all the good it did me. Never liked it over there—the rooms stinking of old paper and no light—not like when the Parfreys were renting. I used to share a dish with that man, when he come in so late at night. It was hard, Sir, to see the low turn that family took.'

'Was it a death?'

'Aye, the father. Accident. And then, two year ago this month it was, Old Man Stannard came back and turned the family out into the hard street. Who knows if they found another? That was your man for you, Sir. They say his house has always told a bad story.'

'He seems to have taken to young Miss Flanner rather well.'

'And the "young", Sir, explains it all. He was the kind of man who never thinks he has time enough in one lifetime. And with a dolly beside him to blow off the loose corns now and then, he could feel himself on his feet again. What I can't see is the likes of that girl coming round with how soon enough she'll have it enough to buy us all. As if Stannard'd had anything to leave for anybody.'

'Has she any other lovers, then?'

'As to that, I couldn't doubt. Why, last month it was, from that very window behind you, Sir, do I see her stopping in the street with her grandfather! It's always the quick ones get the quick, as if there was never no more to us men than a strong leg. But they never have enough, the doxies don't. One is only half as much as two to them.'

'Might I ask, Sir, if either you or Mrs Caddick saw, or heard talk of, the one who came to board up the house? Someone must have remarked it.'

'Nancy was out that day, as I remember, and I was laid up as usual. And my wife had a busy time of it downstairs. I heard the hammering, and then Nancy come up later to tell me about it. And a few days later she passes me the word about the service. It's strange, I warrant, but Drury Lane has seen some stranger sights in its day. Very little can move these people much.'

'I am somewhat surprised that you have not removed yourself from this area. Surely the shutting-up of Stannard's house must suggest to some a return of the plague. And to a man in your condition . . .'

'I've heard that. But if Stannard was taken by the distemper, quitting this house—this very room, Sir— would be the foolishest thing I could do, the infection inhabiting the air as it is said to do. But, as to that, I call it a mighty far chance that the plague should choose to return again to begin at the same address it was said to have began in 'sixty-five. I would hold that Mr Stannard had some little help for himself. And there's some round here knows that better than either of us.'

The house which stood on the other side of Stannard's looked to be one of the oldest in Drury Lane. Its windows were small and misaligned. Years of weekly rains had rounded off its drooping corners. Its door was low and yellowed by the sun. The front had an appearance of changeless permanence, as if the foundations had grown out of the stone of the earth.

The Heath family had owned and lived in the house since the 1650's. The present owner, Alan Heath, worked as a tailor out of a stall in St Martin's Court. He kept his stand six days a week, from early in the morning until sunset. He was not at home when Man made his visit to the house, and the watchman never had the opportunity to meet him.

Of the family's nine children, only two had survived beyond infancy; and now both girls had been married for some time and were living elsewhere with their own families. Man never had the chance to meet them either.

Heath's wife, Amelia, was employed at home as a sewer of books. She was an ascetic-looking woman, with a weak heart and nervous fingers. She seemed to be content with her simple lot in life, quietly satisfied with her honest work, her steady and affectionate husband (the good clothes that she wore had been made by him during his spare hours at night), and her happily settled daughters. She would sit all day at her work-table, her back straight and her lips pursed in concentration.

She welcomed Man into her home and poured him a small glass of ale. As they talked, calmly and as though there were no reason in the world for them to hurry, she continued working at a slow, but methodical pace. Man liked her; she had the same kind of hidden reserves of endurance that he so much valued in his own wife. Theirs was the strength that had so fully become a part of their characters that it was no longer visible as a special quality.

Whatever feelings Amelia Heath may have had about her next-door neighbour, Geoffrey Stannard, had to be inferred by Man through the veil of her habitual politeness and her deference towards one who had been 'important' in the City. She had not seen him often, of course, as he had kept himself lately entirely at home; and, in the days before his move to a better district, he had spent most of his hours in 'Change Alley. Still, within these last two years, she had visited him occasionally to sew up some makeshift volumes of what he called his 'writings': some kind of memoirs, she thought he had mentioned, concerning some time in his past, details from his youth. He had been a great teller of personal stories.

Amelia Heath could not recall any specifics from Stannard's tales—that would be far too disrespectful to the living, not to say the dead—but she had always felt that he talked most about the present or the near, not the distant, past. She somehow had received the impression that he was in some way saving or storing up the experiences of his young manhood—not because they were more secret, but because they were of more potential value. When Man suggested that these were perhaps among the reminiscences recorded in the writings which she herself had been employed to sew up, Amelia Heath delicately insisted that she really could not say if that were true or not. It took Man some minutes to understand that this was the lady's polite manner of informing him that she could not read.

As Man made ready to leave, he heard a cracked voice ranting unintelligibly from somewhere upstairs. Amelia

Heath asked him if he should like to meet her husband's grandmother. It had suddenly occurred to her that the old woman might know something more about the man and the house next door.

Mother Emeny was something of an oddity merely in having managed to survive into her ninety-third year. Blind, deaf, and wandering in the mind, she would sit all day in a shifting patch of sunlight, mumbling incoherently to herself. She looked horribly shrunken, almost caved-in, all but cut off from the outside world. She smelled of age and dust; her mouth drooled; the blank eyes stared out, as if they were straining to see something that had long since died.

Somehow, she had been told of Geoffrey Stannard's death; and, in some private way, Amelia Heath made her understand that there was someone present who wanted to know more about the history of that small part of Drury Lane. Man was told that Mother Emeny had lived in the Heath house for seventy years.

She talked incessantly, as if even unrecognizable speech were the sole human trait remaining to her. Her voice was low and rasping, scorched by age. With careful attention, groups of words, but never complete sentences, could be pieced together and translated into language.

Man sat across from the two women for a full hour. Gradually, he was able to make out, with the help of the younger woman's asides, a crude outline of Mother Emeny's past.

She had married into the Heath household when she was twenty-three. Her husband had been a poor waterman who employed two frequently idle wherries. Alan Heath was her only surviving grandchild. Her own children were now all dead.

In her disordered memory, she was continually confusing Geoffrey Stannard with her husband, who had been drowned during the memorable storm of 1703. Even her recollection of places and events seemed to be unclear: she often referred to the street as Trig Lane and dated the Great Fire after the death of her husband. Listening intently, Man was forced to supplement what she said with what he already knew or had guessed. Many times, he felt himself at a loose end.

Mother Emeny did remember the year of the plague; but, sitting snugly wrapped in a swath of sunlight, the memory seemed not only impossibly distant, but unreal, as if everything had happened to someone else. Amelia Heath added that the old lady sometimes had nightmares of grumbling death-carts and smouldering public coal fires; but that, in the clear light of morning, she quickly forgot. Most of the time, she appeared to be not uncomfortably lost somewhere between the present and the past.

Her husband had, evidently, been one of the few with foresight; and had—early on in the plague year, just after the first rumoured reports of deaths which were said to have been caused by infection—moved himself with his family to one of the free ships sheltering on the Thames. Man automatically asked through Amelia Heath if the grandmother had ever heard the name Coram, but there was no response.

Man tried to focus Mother Emeny's wandering attention on the house in which Geoffrey Stannard had died. Here, her memories seemed slightly more distinct; her dull eyes widened as she struggled towards expression. Stannard had moved in soon after the Fire, that much was fairly clear. But who had lived there before, during the visitation of the plague? Man knew already that there was an inexplicable gap in the rent records for the house during those years. Finally, Mother Emeny was able to recall dimly that there had been a family living there—a man and his wife and, she mumbled, maybe a small boy. The name? Man pressed her as hard as he decently could, but it was no use.

It was like playing a game of chance in the dark. Man guessed at an indistinct word, pieced together a sigh and a nod, elaborated in his own mind the connotations of a shrug. It was tiring work, but he sensed that he might be moving close to something important.

Eventually, Man was able to infer that the mother and the boy had been persuaded to remove with the Heath family to the safety of the ship. The father had remained behind. But, beyond this, the old woman could not be made to tell what had then happened to the mother and the boy, or to the father. She could relate nothing further until Stannard had moved into the house some time after the city had recovered from the two successive disasters and returned to normal. Suddenly she began to repeat— murmuring in the hushed monotone of profound senility— something about a death, a death in the house next door. Man was just starting to feel a revival of his hopes, when he understood that she must at last be referring to the death of Geoffrey Stannard.

Once, as Man was getting up to go, Mother Emeny began to show some animation, as if she were experiencing some unusual emotional reaction to the memories that were running so chaotically through her mind. Her frail body rocked, her colourless eyes filled with tears, she moaned the words 'poor boys, poor boys' in a pained voice. Amelia Heath was able to calm her by smoothing her thin white hair, stroking her head much as Man had stroked the kitten's fur in the chandler's shop. He wondered if the family could have included more than the one son, perhaps an illegitimate child who would be in some way connected to Stannard. But Man had already rejected that possibility, and now the grandmother was too spent and confused to be of any more help to him.

Amelia Heath kindly invited Man to return when her husband would be at home, although she was sure he would not be able to provide any more information than she and the old woman.

Man left her at her work-table, a calm and competent woman who held to the simple values of her life and did not want for more. In a few hours, her husband would settle down to a solid meal and a good pipe and some quiet companionship in the front parlour before bedtime.

And, in an upper room, Mother Emeny would be continuing her tireless monologue in the dark.

Man could learn absolutely nothing from Geoffrey Stannard's more fashionable residence in Bedford Row. The house was new and clean, with an airy brightness that contrasted sharply with the other in Drury Lane. The stone shone brightly, even in the shadow cast by the sun's setting behind it. The street was quiet. The few people walking along it were well-dressed and respectable.

How sweet a triumph it must have seemed to Stannard to have managed by his own talents to escape from the fetid closeness of Drury Lane to such a pleasurable retreat with the open spaces of Lamb's Conduit Fields stretching northward. It would have represented the crowning justification of years of ignominy and struggle.

Yet it would have made the shameful return to Drury Lane a doubly bitter defeat. No wonder the man had, in his last years, been driven frantic in his need to regain the heights which he surely believed were his proper place.

Now the fine house was empty, a formal 'To Let' notice fixed on the street door. The neighbours on either side were new. Man could find no one in Bedford Row who could tell him anything of much significance about Stannard's nine-year stay in the neighbourhood. In this part of town, the people were more reserved and maintained a more dignified distance from one another. Man himself felt out of his element.

As he turned towards home, he told himself that he had no reason to feel discouraged. The day had not proved to be a complete waste of time. He knew that in a pocket of his greatcoat he carried a copy of the official inventory of the total contents of the house in which Geoffrey Stannard had been murdered. And he knew, too, that on that list was made no mention of any volumes of memoirs which Amelia Heath had worked so diligently to bind.

CHAPTER 5

There was always something about the cold winds and early darkness of October that gave Sarah Man a feeling of pleasant melancholy. In the mornings she looked forward to doing her marketing. She would go out to brave the icy air and to watch the breaths of the crowds plume brightly in the cold sunlight. In the late afternoons she would sit at the window with her sewing, settled in the gathering dark. Better to be able to hear her husband snoring roundly in the next room or rustling the pages of a journal from his deep chair; but it was enough for her to know that, even if he were out, he would be somewhere in London and, at times, probably thinking of her. Worst was at night, before sleep came, the street and the house both black, every creak and bump magnified, her mind worrying some thought like a loose thread, wondering down which empty street Man was turning now . . .

It had been the same for eighteen years, but she knew she would never get used to it.

It was so much better, now that the boy had come. Toby had been with them for nearly a month. He was stronger and happier; and now Sarah had someone else's breathing, added to her own, to listen for at night — a

soft, open-mouthed sigh coming from the short bed they
had set up in a corner of their room. But sometimes it was
not good for her to listen to it for too long.

During the days, she would take him shopping and let
him carry home the heaviest parcels. After dinner, she
would teach him his letters; then he and Man, if he were
at home, would trade recollections of London street-life.
The boy seemed to know as much as her husband about
what went on in the narrow lanes and alleys of the city. It
frightened her: sometimes the boy knew too much.

They had made the few required official inquiries
concerning the whereabouts of the boy's father with no
success. Toby himself could tell them little about any
surviving family. As far as he could remember, both his
sister and his brother were dead. Sarah knew, as well as
her husband, that there was no good place to send him;
yet she lived in daily fear that something might happen to
take the boy away.

She had really not thought much of this Captain
Thomas Coram, who had stopped in once and sat for
hours with her husband in earnest conversation. His ideas
were certainly sincere and ambitious, but he seemed to
her altogether too gruff and muscular to direct the
welfare of so many children. Even her husband, as gentle
a man as he was, could not bring quite the right kind of
tenderness to such work. They were too practical and
businesslike. A woman was what was needed.

Man had been trying, during the last month, to give as
much of his time as he could to her and the boy; but his
regular duties filled his nights, and the death of Geoffrey
Stannard had come to consume his days. He slept so little.
She had rarely seen him so caught up in such an incident.
She wondered if there must be some special quality about
this murder that would not let him rest.

He had talked to her about it, as he did with almost all
his work. Sometimes Man was too close to the scene, too

deeply immersed in the dramatic life of the streets;
sometimes it had coloured his perspective on human
nature. Then, he would come to her for the fresh insights
of one who is involved only in the normal difficulties of
everyday living.

This time, he had shared less with her than usual. He
seemed to be almost personally disturbed by Stannard's
death, as though it had touched him in some private way.
It was not unlike him to be moved to pity or rage by the
misfortunes or inhumanity of others; but now his efforts
to come to an understanding of the people and the events
were weighted with the urgency of a man who wants
mostly to understand himself. His wife felt it was not that
he would not tell her more about the work, but that he
could not.

About a week after the discovery of Stannard's body,
the two of them had been talking beside the fire, half-
listening to the boy at the table learning his lesson and to
a late-afternoon rain lashing violently against the
window. It was raining so fiercely that even Man had
decided to stay indoors until it let up.

Sarah had just remarked, over her ceaseless sewing,
that at least one could not call Stannard's death untimely:
the very old must be prepared to die at any time. Whereas
the poor young ones, who die before they have a chance
to live . . .

Man had interrupted her, disagreeing.

'Yet somehow I feel the tragedy of Mr Stannard's case
more. He was, by most accounts, a hard man and a selfish
one. But here is a man who spends a lifetime striving for
success—a lonely success that must take the place of wife
and family—only to lose everything at an age when few
men could even think of starting again. Yet I understand
that he does try, frantically, to begin again, to try to raise
himself a second time out of the slough of Drury Lane.
And then he is cut off, brutally, by enforced starvation,

perhaps just as he is making ready his final triumph.'

'What was it, then, that he was working at?'

'No man knows. My thought is that the collapse of the South Sea venture might finally have dissuaded him, as it did many, from further speculation. Before moving to Bedford Row, he was known to be methodical and persistent in his business affairs; but after the fall, he seemed to be too desperately hurried to endure the slow uncertainties of finance. I have learned that, for these past two years, he has not been heard of in the City. I suspect that he may have been planning to try a direction completely different from any he had ever taken before.'

'But what new career could a man turn to, so late in life, that would promise some profit? I can't think what you would do, Sir, if you were to quit the watch, and you're but half his age.'

She had regarded her husband with quiet affection as he sat smoking his pipe. He was looking into the fire, as if the flames could show him a glimpse of what he was looking for.

At the table, the boy could be seen nodding over his book. The noisy wind and rain seemed to cut the three of them off from the rest of the world, but the fire kept them warm and safe.

'A man who survives to the age of eighty has much experience, many useful memories behind him. Perhaps he had seen something years ago that he found only now could be put to use. And necessity would be an added impetus. Or it may be that he had known someone who could now be of help to him. As yet, we know very little of the friends and acquaintances he must have had after so many active years in his work.'

'Has no one spoken out?'

'By Mr Jessop's direction, the death of Mr Stannard has come to be regarded as more or less natural. Besides, many of Stannard's age must be long since gone. As you remarked, death at such an age is more expected than not. And who can say but that one who knew Stannard long ago, or knew him well these many years, has not harboured an old grievance against him? Enmity endures as long as friendship, often longer.'

'You seem, Sir, to be looking mainly to the past for your answers.'

Man had considered this with his usual quiet determination, his gaze fixed somewhere before the fire. As he reached for a straw to relight his pipe, he had spoken with a strange calmness.

'To kill a fellow human being in such a distinctive and horrid fashion bespeaks a profound hatred. And hatred always has a very long history.'

Since that afternoon, Sarah Man knew only that her husband had been spending all his free hours visiting the many pawnshops and receivers scattered throughout the city, searching for some trace of Stannard's writings. She could not understand what he hoped to gain by finding it. At times, he seemed to be less concerned with Stannard's death than with his life, with the intricacies of his hidden past.

She was worried about his health. His cold had worsened; what little sleep he did take was broken by a dry, painful cough. The weather was wet and cold; the nights were freezing. When he came home in the early morning, he would be shivering and stiff with cold and weariness, his hands chapped and blue. Occasionally, he would not stop in at all during the day, only sending a message by way of a friend or a tradesman to tell her he was not injured or in danger.

And there was still the boy to be considered. She had seen her husband looking at Toby with a peculiar wistfulness which she could not comprehend, as if the separate concerns of Stannard's past and the boy's future were somehow related.

In the declining October light, she sat thoughtful and anxious, sensing the approach of still another winter.

Of Isaac Hervey it had been said that he was fit to live nowhere but a gaol. The speaker was Hervey's father, an irascible patriarch who was fond of criticizing those very qualities which he had worked so hard in passing on to his only son. He had long ago disowned him, but he found it far more difficult to ignore him. The son's notoriety pursued the father: total strangers stopped him in the street with demands for debts no man could pay with honour. Publicly, the old man blackguarded his son with vehemence; but privately, in the seclusion of his study, he wagged his head in secret delight over the prodigal exploits of his one-time heir.

Isaac Hervey was twenty-five years of age, handsome and glib, an inveterate borrower, self-pitying and reckless, capable of prodigious feats of drinking. He was also resolute and caring, a man whose ultimate loyalty — once given — could never be called in doubt. Man had known him since he was a boy, wildly ranging through the streets of London. He had more than once brought Hervey to the watch-house and had as often turned a blind eye to his more minor indiscretions. Man had seen him parading in a scarlet cloak with gold lace and his naked toes peeking through his ruined shoes; and he had also had occasion to thank him for helping to hold off a band of club-swinging ruffians.

Hervey was one of those who could never truly be said to be working at anything. He had no steady source of income, other than the good will of those who knew and appreciated him — or tolerated him. He was sometime watchman, sometime speculator, sometime informer. He was never employed, but never idle. Man valued most his encyclopaedic knowledge of the city's underworld — its internal logic, its changing associations, its disguised contacts with so-called 'legitimate' society. No one knew his way through the mazes of London's poor and criminal better than Hervey. Man had often said that Hervey could identify the character of any stratum of low-life by smell alone.

Man thought first of Hervey, when he had decided to follow the track of Stannard's missing writings. On his first free night, he walked over Holborn Hill and turned into the squalor of Field Lane, where this week Hervey kept a night-cellar. Hervey moved about often, sometimes daily, depending on the urgency of his poverty or the enthusiasm of his creditors.

The night was windless, and the dampness of the air weighed down upon the narrow lane. There were few streets in London which could equal the reeking stench that struck Man full in the face as he continued northward. The intersecting channel of the Fleet ditch churned with the cast-away offal of the tripe-dressers, sausage-makers and catgut-spinners who shared the lane with the native assortment of professional thieves. The total degradation of the area depressed Man, and he threaded his way among beggars and hawkers and sleepy link-boys with feelings of anger and helplessness.

Isaac Hervey's single-room night-cellar was located half way up the street. Along the way, Man passed by others which housed greengrocers, cobblers and tippling dens. He had been told that Hervey's was next to a milk walk, which he finally recognized by the pails and wooden tallies piled up in front of the entrance. The milk cellar's flap was shut for the night, and a hairless dog was busy lapping at the crusted foam that had formed on the rims of the pails.

The flap of the well beside the milk walk was missing. Broken stone steps led down into a shadowed, airless cavity. Man felt for each step with his toe, as he gingerly descended into the dark.

He walked directly into a box of a room in which a tall man like Hervey could not stand erect. The few bits of furnishings were uniformly colourless: a small wainscot table with uneven legs; two unsafe chairs with cane bottoms; a squat iron stove; a brass pint pot and a cracked stone teacup spilling salt. In a corner, across a low sagging bed, was stretched the loose figure of Isaac Hervey, asleep.

Man wondered again if the young man lived in such places out of necessity or preference. He had noted before, in the errant sons of successful fathers, this tendency to seek out a life which was the exact opposite of that which had been so carefully prepared for them. In Hervey's case, he actually seemed to relish the lowest and most depraved levels of society. It had been often said of Isaac Hervey that he was deliberately acting out the adventures which his father had always contemplated, but never dared.

Young Hervey did not appear particularly surprised to find Man bending over him. They had not seen each other for nearly six months, but Hervey was used to Man's calling on him at odd times for help. He had heard of Geoffrey Stannard's death and of Man's interest in it, as he seemed to hear of everything that went on in the city.

Man looked down with a smile at the half-awake face.

'I need you, Sir, to help me find something that may or may not have been stolen.'

For the next three weeks, during as many hours as they could spare, the two men toured the almost infinite number of pawnshops, fences, occasional purchasers, habitual receivers, and various known locks buried in the most secretive corners of the poorest sections of London. Taking Drury Lane as their point of departure, they worked outward in concentric circles towards the borders where the congested streets finally gave way to open fields. The task seemed endless. They could afford to overlook no place, however small or innocent in appearance, into which a man might conceivably turn in the hope of profitably ridding himself of stolen goods. The private writings of a man who had once been of some wealth and of some reputation in the City could fetch a good price; and, if the pages should contain anything at all scandalous or newsworthy, the asking price could be raised considerably. Yet trading in stolen papers was always a hazardous, though lucrative and widespread, business. In this case, unless the thief were of roughly the same age as Stannard, he could not brazenly present the writings as his own. He would be forced to resort to only the most disreputable, or the most illiterate, of receivers.

During their ranging search together, Man and Hervey speculated about the theft of Stannard's memoirs. Had the murderer known about the makeshift volumes before he entered the house? Was there something about the subject-matter contained within the pages that was itself significant? Yet, if securing the writings had been the main motive for the killing, why had Stannard been put to death in such a ritualistic manner, resembling a purposeful execution? Or did the man who had posed for a moment in the street as Stannard's son have some totally separate reason for his crime, only discovering the pages by sheer accident?

By tacit consent, neither Man nor Hervey suggested that Stannard himself might have disposed of the manuscript long before his death, in which case all their present efforts must be in vain.

For nearly three weeks, they were disappointed by the indifference of tired old men in dingy shops, rejected by furtive boys new to the trade, and once set upon by an offended businesswoman who kept a stall of old clothes in Monmouth Street. Most were reluctant to speak to men who wore the mark, if not always the uniform, of the watch. This was one of the reasons that Man had thought to bring Isaac Hervey along with him: the young man had the gift of making himself appear to be one of the underworld's own. Man could seem at times too authoritative, too powerfully insistent.

Just as Man noticed that his companion was beginning to lose interest in their tedious work, their luck changed. One night, they stepped into one of the arched doorways beneath the twin towers of King Street Gate to shelter from a stinging gust of wind. Beside them, a blind man stood leaning against the wall with his hat held out open before him. He was doing a brisk trade; the cold had not succeeded in diminishing the traffic passing through the Gate in great waves of steaming horses and of muttering crowds.

Isaac Hervey blew into his cupped hands.

'There's talk of pulling this Gate down soon. 'Tis said to be an obstruction to traffic.' He pressed himself against the wall to make way for a cartload of fowl, then looked at the heavy stonework over his head. 'Still, it does cut down some on the wind's running along the street.'

He turned to Man, who wore a thoughtful look on his face.

'What is it, friend? Are we to quit the night, then?'

Man shook himself and smiled weakly.

'I was only thinking of the rôle the South Sea scandal played in the sequence that led to the sudden death of Geoffrey Stannard. And quite near to where we now stand, as you may know, lies Queen Square, the owner of which is Sir Theodore Jannsen, a chief promoter of that ill-fated scheme. I wonder how much longer he will be able to enjoy the possession of it.'

They turned their backs to the wind and continued down King Street. Before they reached the dark mass of Westminster Abbey, just past the entrance into Thieving Lane, they turned right into the Little Sanctuary. Here, the Gothic houses arched their pointed gables over the street until they almost met as one overhead. From a few windows, soiled sheets still hung wet and limp from jutting poles. At one place, a miscellaneous collection of furniture stood in the middle of the way: a tall-backed chair, a winged table with a few empty bottles strewn on top, a cracked oval mirror in which the image of the two men split and passed. Worn women and haggard men milled aimlessly about.

As soon as they stepped into the street, two or three boys broke away from small groups and began to run from place to place down the road, shouting a few indistinguishable words. Man knew them to be the area's own watchers, who were now hurrying to inform the inhabitants of the intrusion of the two watchmen. This was unavoidable, the Little Sanctuary being a closed community within the city with its own harsh and exclusive laws. Man felt Hervey tense beside him, and he himself wished he had not chosen this night to leave his staff behind. Not everyone who entered this neighbourhood came out.

Eventually, they stood looking up at an iron spear that extended outward from above a scrolled doorway. From the spear hung an inverted cross, upon the points of which were fixed three iron balls. A smeared signboard read: 'W. Mason Pawn Broker.' A woman dressed in a torn shirt was about to enter the shop, carrying two tarnished pots and a pair of bent tongs.

Man turned to his young friend.

'Is this the place you have heard such report about?'

'Aye, but I make no promises.'

The interior of the shop was the kind of meaningless jumble of broken utensils and unusable refuse that could only be expected. Man noted the unmatched pairs of shoes, the gaudily bound prayer-books and testaments, fans of displayed spoons, cards of rings and brooches, curling prints of moonlit Spanish landscapes. The atmosphere was cramped and discouraging.

W. Mason was a lean dry gnome of a man, whose thin mouth curved downward at one corner. He stared at his two visitors unhappily.

'What's the merchandise, gen'men?'

Man hung back, while Isaac Hervey stepped briskly forward.

'Friend of mine, old cove of a bookstall, was in low water the other time, dodged in here to drop a bundle of papers. Now he's sent me in with the ribband.'

The broker's sallow eyes shifted from Hervey towards the shadowy figure of Man, who had kept back out of the light of the counter-lamp.

'Letters? Pamphlets? Tracts? Notes? What?'

He seemed unusually suspicious, as if he feared being found in possession of something dangerous.

'His memoirs it was, or so he told me. Biggish, handbound, well-writ. My friend's an educated man. Never set my eyes on it myself, though.'

The outline of Mason's sickly body relaxed, as if the tension in a rope had been released. He waved a limp hand in the direction of vague stacks of books and magazines.

'We've plenty of spare paper on hand. But what's your friend's name? Where's his claim? You can't redeem without a rightful claim.'

Man moved up to face the pawnbroker and rested the fingers of his right hand on the counter-top, looking studiously down at them.

'The writings are substantial, in two or three volumes. Cheap paper, common ink, but very carefully sewn. The hand is old, but firm and decisive. The text, if I remember rightly, deals with events of nearly sixty years past. Something about the Great Plague, I think. It would have been offered some time during the past three or four weeks, possibly by some man of about your age.

You may have thought our friend seemed to be in something of a hurry.'

None of the three men was deceived by the pretence; but, in such dealings between parish officials and members of the underground society of thieves and receivers, the indirect method was silently agreed upon as the best.

W. Mason was suddenly struck by a surprising thought, or he pretended to be so. On their part, Man and Hervey tried not to appear too anxious, feigning an impatient indifference.

'I mind a certain party come in here but a night or so ago. Right nervous and eager for the rhino, with a load of such papers as you've marked. Ready to take any amount o' bite for them. I said as I don't trade in the private script much—there's trouble there—but I was insisted upon. So I takes my look, and then I elect to give it the go-by. The stuff's worth a stretch on the stalls right now, but what am I to do with it? Grub Street's, I said, but a mile away.'

Man had the impression that the broker had indeed been greatly interested in the writings, but that he had for some reason—perhaps fear—shied away from accepting them.

'Was the man, then, an older gentleman? Somewhat poor in look, worried or in haste?'

'What man are we about? I never spoke the half of that. Young girl, very. Polite and all, served me right well she did.'

Man and Hervey drew closer together, exchanging a look. Man spoke quickly to the pawnbroker.

'What was the look of her?'

'Young, pretty, like all the rest of them, ready to do it all for you. Makes one want to have been born a few later.'

'Did she say her name?'

'No need to. We'd no business.'

The street door opened and a boy came in, holding a child's rumpled nightdress. The broker made an exasperated gesture towards the two men. Man noted a tone of anger and frustration mixed with fear.

'But you can find her as well as any. I've seen her before, in certain company. Everyone knows her to be one of him what's made it harder for the rest of us. She's one of Wild's fine morts.'

Man was alone the next day when he paid a visit to Wild's large business office at the Sign of King Charles the First's Head in the Great Old Bailey, close to the prison. Hervey had said that he had no taste for calling on the man whom the newspaper advertisements described as 'Thief-Catcher-General of Great-Britain and Ireland.' Man suspected that Hervey's aversion was less civic than personal, and that his young friend must in some way have come up against Wild's formidable corporation of thieves, conveyers and informers.

For Man himself, in a career extending over twenty-seven years, some contact with Wild's city-wide organization had been inevitable. The two men had met and talked a half-dozen times in the past, neither being especially impressed by the other. Man had known of Wild since the latter's more modest early days, when he was associated with Mary Milliner—a pickpocket who looked more like a crow than a woman—in the operation of a brothel in Lewkenor's Lane, and then of a public house in Cock Alley, Cripplegate. For his part, Wild considered the watchman to be annoyingly impractical and idealistic. But he knew, too, that Man needed to be reckoned with: certain members of his gangs had already fallen into Man's hands.

Sitting in Wild's ornately furnished parlour, Man studied his host's opulently laced coat and glanced at the silver staff of authority, set importantly in a gilt stand.

He could not help but compare it to the crude wooden watchman's staff that he had left out in the front hall.

Wild's heavy face was set and grim. Man knew him to be about forty years of age, but thought he looked considerably older. The slackened skin suggested a history of dissipation.

Frail sunlight shone through a window and glinted off a garish buckle, worn as an ironic comment on Wild's first profession.

'You seek me out, Sir, in connection with the death of this man — what's the name? — Geoffrey Stannard? I had heard it reported that he died of some sudden illness. Why do you then wish to concern me with this affair? Am I a physician?'

Man took his time in replying.

'You are, Sir, as all the town knows, our foremost recoverer of what is termed "lost" property. And, as Mr Hitchin's pamphlet of a few years past contended, our chief architect and instigator of these same losses. It was, therefore, to your counsel, Sir, that I thought first to turn, when I learned of the papers missing from Mr Stannard's home.'

The other was too well aware of his powerful position in the city, in high stations as well as low, to feel the disapproval of a mere watchman.

'I have replied to Charles Hitchin's black charges in print. As for your inquiry, you have done well to come to me. I do a most successful business here in the recovery of private papers. Usually,' he continued, glancing wickedly over Man's simple and worn clothes, 'only the better class of gentlemen seek my advice. I may say that Lord Raymond himself has lately been most satisfied with my work. All quite discreetly, of course.'

Man met the other's look with calm assurance.

'As you say, Sir, the theft of such papers has in these times become too common amongst us. This is known by all; but how exactly does your office serve in such a loss?'

Wild reached towards the floor and brought up a bottle and two short glasses. He held the glasses by two darkened fingers thrust inside. He poured for himself and left the other standing empty on the table. Man sat without moving, placidly nursing the pipe he had lit upon first sitting down. He seemed determined to fill the sumptuous room as thickly as possible with bitter smoke.

Wild propped his elbows on the table, holding his glass up to cover his mouth as he spoke. From his voice, Man had already guessed that he had probably been drinking most of the day.

'As you know, such personal papers have value only for the owner — the memoranda of the statesman, the figures of the speculator upon 'Change, the manuscripts of the scribbler. The thief himself knows that the highest bid will come from his victim, or from that man's representative. You may read, Sir, notices in the news-sheets every day, announcing a reward for the return of some papers — of vast concern to the writer alone — with a promise of no questions asked. But this is an uncertain and risk-filled course: any sum can be demanded and will be paid, with no real guarantee that the goods will be restored. The wise and cautious gentleman comes to me first. My own advertisements obtain surer results. I know this city as few men can; I have hundreds in my employ to search out the stolen property; and I can safely settle a just exchange of merchandise and money. The owner himself can stand apart. I do all the work, take all the hazards, and ask only a reasonable commission.'

Man knew, as well as any, the extent and effectiveness of Wild's operations. By means of cleverness and ruthlessness, Wild had managed to perfect a system by which he set himself up as the indispensable conduit between the most respectable circles of London society and the ubiquitous underworld. Publicly, he enjoyed a dubious reputation as a restorer of stolen valuables and as a prosecutor of the lawless. In truth—and as all knew, but few dared admit—he arranged first, through his network of gangs, the theft of those same items which he was later hired to recover and summarily informed against any who resisted his command. There was no one in London who better manipulated both the innocent and the felon.

It was just such as Wild with whom Man felt the deepest bitterness, yet against whom he knew he was most powerless to act.

He drew softly on his pipe and watched critically the proud man sitting before him. How much longer, thought Man, can his reign endure?

Wild waited for the watchman to speak.

'But, in the example of Mr Stannard—whom we now believe to have been put to death with great calculation—the thief could expect to earn nothing from the bartering of any private papers. The man left neither family nor friends, and no one can collect from the dead. Yet his writings are gone—three large volumes, well-bound, of personal reflections. Now how is this to be explained?'

Wild revolved his glass between his fingers, staring at it thoughtfully. This would appear to be something entirely new to his experience.

'I would expect the papers had some native significance, known only to the thief. It may have been something of which even the owner himself was unaware.'

Man considered this seriously for a moment, letting his pipe burn itself out in his hand. His head ached from too little sleep. His mouth was parched, but he had no intention of helping himself to the bottle and glass set in front of Wild.

'You tell me, Sir, that you have working for you a main force of people to aid you in your search for information and for goods. I presume, then, you number some women among them.'

'Of course. Much of what goes forward in this town concerns women even more largely than men.'

'And would some of these women be engaged, directly or indirectly, in the domestic services?'

Wild's corporation of thieves was partitioned into nearly autonomous gangs, to each of which was allotted a specific type of labour. One patrolled the major roads into London; one mingled among the congregations of churches, another among the crowds at entertainments and public functions, especially the madly popular hangings at Tyburn; and a special brigade was trained and let out as domestics. And these comprised only the most active segments. There were also the disguised warehouses for storage, the watchmakers and the jewel-workers for necessary alterations, and the watermen with their sloops for long-range transport. Few legitimate business enterprises and no public offices could boast of such model organization.

Wild delayed in giving his answer, possibly worrying about where all this was leading.

'Not a few. Such women are best placed to make the closest report of the theft.' He paused and looked slyly across at Man. 'At times, they themselves may become involved in the very act — as observers, naturally.'

'Do any of your acquaintance happen to reside or work in the vicinity of Drury Lane?'

Now, Wild's instinctive caution and distrust of parish officials were definitely roused. He sat back and spoke in a slow, careful voice.

'As you must be aware, Sir, Drury Lane is one of our most notorious areas. I would be called simple if I did not have one or two young women well-placed in that street.'

'You know one Nancy Flanner, then?'

'A good enough girl for her age. Don't trust too much

in what is sometimes said of her. If she has a failing, it is
that she is perhaps too ready to give of herself. She would
go without to meet the need of another. And that's
Christian, I will say, more so than some.'

It was getting late. The room was beginning to darken
by degrees. Man decided it was time to press Wild for
more useful details.

'I should tell you, Mr Wild, that this same Nancy
Flanner is suspected of having tried to dispose of some
papers at a pawnbroker's shop in Westminster. These, I
believe, represent the missing volumes of Geoffrey
Stannard. The girl lives and works, as you may already
know, in a chandler's shop next to Stannard's house, and
was known to be intimately connected with him. These
circumstances suggest, I think, that Miss Flanner may
well have played some part in the original theft or in the
murder or in both. I fear that her acquaintances may no
longer be considered associates, but accessories.'

Wild stood up awkwardly and took an unsteady turn
about the room. As he passed behind Man, his hip grazed
against the back of the watchman's chair. By the time he
had returned to the table, all traces of drink had gone
from his voice and manner.

'Hear me, Watchman. If there be any truth in what
you say, then you must go and speak to Nancy Flanner
herself. She may be able to supply you with a perfectly
lawful explanation of her actions. If she did indeed know
this man Stannard as well as you say, then it is possible, is
it not, that before his death he made a present of his
writings to her. If this is the case, then she is free to do
with them what she will.'

'And yet, in conversation with me,' said Man, 'held
before I learned of the missing volumes, she made no
mention of Stannard's having been at work upon his
memoirs—a detail of which she could not easily have
been ignorant, knowing him as well as she did. Now that I

know somewhat more about the situation, I intend to question the girl again this evening. I wished first to see you, Sir, to ask you if she is currently at work in Drury Lane on your behalf.'

Wild looked narrowly at Man, trying to judge how seriously the watchman wanted to implicate him in this affair.

'I may say that she has done some small chores for me in the past, both there and elsewhere. A letter missing, some jewellery misplaced, untrustworthy domestics—nothing very great. But I have not, I can assure you, seen the girl these two months. If she has somehow involved herself in this offence, in either a legal or an illegal manner, I will not have any of it laid to me. I will not, Sir!'

Man noticed that Wild had begun gradually to show more feeling in his efforts to clear himself. But even here, so great was Wild's confidence in his own supremacy, he seemed to feel not a fear of finding himself personally exposed to danger, but an anger at the presumption of one of his gang's daring to work independently of his control. Wild had a dark history of dealing swiftly and horribly with any deserters from his camp.

As for Nancy Flanner's true association with the gangs, it was not difficult for Man to imagine her place in the scheme of things. He had little doubt but that Wild had been planning some important theft in Drury Lane—probably from either Caddick's or Stannard's house—and had stationed the girl there to review and report. Some minor thieving might already have been committed, only to be settled in secrecy according to the usual methods. If Wild had been looking forward to something bigger—perhaps a series of robberies, spaced out over the course of a year—he would still have wanted to keep Nancy Flanner on the scene in the guise of a simple servant. This could help to explain his present wrath: now, he would have to have her replaced.

Yet Man was as certain of Wild's innocence—if he could call it that—regarding the Stannard theft and murder as he was of Nancy Flanner's direct involvement. The taking of valuable papers was one of Wild's many trademarks; but the unnecessary murder, as well as the peculiar manner in which the killing had been arranged, were bothersome complications which seemed uncharacteristic of his rough temperament. And, as Man knew, even the most violent and lawless follow some consistent patterns of their own.

By this time, Man fully believed that today was the first Wild had heard of the girl's recent activities. Yet Man needed to know more, particularly about her friends and contacts; he could not imagine for a moment that she had acted alone.

'Am I to take your meaning then to be that Nancy Flanner was working entirely on her own in this instance?'

'A show of individualism which I trust she will soon come to regret, if she had thought to concern me in such a double felony as this. My sometime association with the girl obliges her to keep faith with me and not to drag me down with her into common crimes. My work here is built upon trust, and I have no idea to hazard it for the like of Nancy Flanner.'

Wild set both his large hands palm down upon the table, but he did not even reach for the half-emptied bottle. The room was so quiet that Man could hear a distant rumbling in Wild's throat. The man behind the table—now a dense bulk of shadow—seemed to loom larger against the background of the grey window.

One of Wild's servants—a slovenly, crooked youngster whom Man thought was still in prison—stepped apologetically into the room, set a shaded candle on the table, and left. Now, Man could see Wild's almost black eyes fixed squarely upon him as a heated flush crept shade by shade into the 'thief-catcher's' face.

'To speak plainly with you, Sir, Miss Flanner is nothing much above the commonest fen in London. She is famous among the canters in this city only for her taste for the old fumblers and for being so full of herself that she's quite well empty. She comes from a low enough line on the river, mixed with every sort of Frenchified blood that's been cast ashore. And it's all the girl can do to read her own name! She once even had the face to act the wife to me — me that lost an infant boy up at Wolverhampton the very year, I don't doubt, that she was born.'

At this, Man felt a stirring of his own anger. He had heard enough stories of Wild's beginnings in Wolverhampton and of the son who had lost the father.

'I shouldn't think, Sir —'

'The worst of it being I got damn little good work out of her. What time she doesn't spend firkytoodling the master she's out running with these garreteer friends of hers. And there's nothing to be got out of them, I've told her that more than twice; what they have most of is what nobody needs — nothing! If it's paper and Flanner you want to see together, Sir, I would send you off to them scribblers with the empty pockets. They can tell you more of what you want to know — for the price of a glass or a dish!'

He pointed a bent finger at Man's chest.

'Mark me, Sir. What Nancy Flanner does is no more part of me. I'm well off that one. She'll ride a pony foaled on an acorn before me!'

It was quite dark now. Man would come late to his work. As he walked away from Wild's office, through the crowd milling about before the prison, he was hoping he would still be able to find the time in the early night to stop in at the chandler's shop for another talk with the girl.

For some reasons he could explain and for a few he

could not, Man could accept easily the relative sincerity of both Wild's statements and his anger. The 'Thief-Catcher-General' was at once too simple and too smart to entangle himself in such a scheme with such an accomplice.

And in two days' time, at his second visit to the office in the Old Bailey, Man had no hesitation in believing Wild when he insisted that he had had no hand in Nancy Flanner's disappearing from the shop in Drury Lane — and, it seemed, from all of London — at approximately the same hour as their first interview.

CHAPTER 6

All the talk in the tavern had something or other to do with writing: verses on the imagined virtues of some sought-after patron; articles to be written on order and ahead of deadlines on subjects of absolutely no interest to the writer; multi-volumed catalogues and histories which would demand the labour of years with only the vaguest promises of future rewards. Here some spoke of the best rates for new subscriptions; there, of two translators at work upon the same text, each frantic to get into print before the other. Everywhere was talk about the necessity of speed and quantity: fifteen hundred words per hour, eighteen columns between noon and sunset, forty of the printed octavo pages at a single sitting.

The clientele, otherwise as various as any in London, all had one thing in common: they each bore the appearance of real and chronic need. What coats did not look threadbare looked borrowed. Most of the faces were young, but thin and lined. A dozen were crowded close about the fire, as though this might be the only heat they would feel this week. Food and drink were ordered against payment expected from tomorrow's issue of a newspaper. Names of brokers were exchanged — those with whom one could pawn the first few pages of a book, retrieve them by pawning the next, and so on until the end. Collaborations were devised, the identities of anonymous contributors were debated, the best known editors were abused for their ignorance and their stinginess. At every table, the talk revolved solely upon the current price of words.

Man had begun to feel at home in the company of these castaways who lived and worked in and around Grub Street. By now, he had talked with quite a number of them about Nancy Flanner and about what might have become of three sizeable volumes of unedited memoirs. Among the garreteers and hack-writers, opinions were exchanged as promiscuously as quotations; Man was able to gather a great deal of hearsay and personal impressions, but little reliable information. No one knew anything of such a large manuscript's circulating among the publishers and booksellers. And the few who had heard of the young girl and of those men with whom she may have been seen could give Man no particulars — or would not. In its own way, the society of Grub Street was as closed and self-protective as that of the Little Sanctuary and fully as reluctant to share its confidences with an outsider, especially with a minor parish officer.

It had been a long, hard week for Man. Nothing had been learned of Nancy Flanner since she had innocently stepped out of the shop with a bag to run an errand. Her mother in Wapping could only wonder what had happened in the last few months to the money her daughter was used to send and — as an afterthought — to the daughter she had not laid eyes on since the spring. No one had seen the girl receive any message prior to leaving. No unknown body had been reported found. Man, as always, feared the worst.

And then the boy, Toby, had been taken by a high fever. Now, when Man came home in the morning, his wife looked even more haggard than he, having sat up all night long watching over the boy's broken sleep. During part of the day, Man was kept busy trying to coax Toby into eating some soup or reading to him or cooling his face as he rested beside Sarah. A physician had visited the house; but his advice was so evasive, and his fee so high, that he could not well be trusted. Sarah imagined the darkest — an inflammation on the brain — and Man could not help but share her dread.

His work, too, had lately become even more dangerous. Roving bands of drunken men had begun terrorizing the St Giles area. They were all armed and fearless; they had already robbed a score of citizens and beaten one old watchman nearly to death. Man knew it was an added worry for his wife. Usually, she could sleep during his absence and not have to think too much; but now, sitting up with the boy, she had long hours to spend in the quiet darkness of the house, alone with her fears.

Man thought about his home now, as he sat in the busy Grub Street tavern. This evening he was sharing a corner table with a young man of twenty-four named Jack Ellis. He was a thin and unassuming youth, serious and modest, with a manner that was at once confident and apologetic. Man had soon learned that Ellis was an odd combination of practicality and creativity. As a career, he was in training in Threadneedle Street to become a money-scrivener; but he was also most dedicated to the writing of poetry and to the study of his beloved Ovid's *Epistles*. Two years earlier, his poem, 'The South Sea Dream', had been well received; yet he continued to be so excessively self-effacing that he sincerely had no real desire to publish his work. Man guessed him to be mechanically meticulous in his daily work and passionately devoted to his avocation.

He was evidently a quick learner and got on well with his associates, both in the offices of finance and in the coffee houses of the literary world. He had also known Geoffrey Stannard.

'An interesting man, Mr Stannard, if I may be allowed the word. Quite old, of course, when I knew him during the South Sea fiasco. Too bad for him really, it was all out of his hands, he had no selection in the matter. Quite demolished him it did, in an emotional sense, I mean. At his age, I expect he could not think he had any options left. You may say he was hardly alone: I did, in fact, know of many who had lost as much as he, or more. But most of them had the strength—or somehow found it—to come back. With Stannard, there was first his advanced years to be considered; and then he seemed to have entertained such an unnatural confidence in his financial dealings. I suppose that a man does not wish to see his work of a lifetime come to nought, especially if he has no wife or family to comfort him. But his kind are, after all, named "speculators". A man of his experience should have been better prepared for the turnings of Dame Fortune.'

'Did you talk with him much at the time?'

The young man squinted his close-set eyes in an effort to remember. He would be the kind who prides himself on accurate recollection.

'Well, yes. Once we ate together at a small house behind the Royal Exchange. This was, I believe, at about the time when the numbers had begun to turn very bad indeed. Most of us knew what was coming, although we could not imagine that it was going to be as bad as it was. There's always that in the business, you know: the trends are usually quite clear, but what surprises you is their severity.'

Man looked closely at Jack Ellis and thought that here was one who, for all his perfectly genuine modesty, would be less often surprised than most.

'I recall that Stannard appeared to be pretty well panicked at his prospects. He had settled nearly all of his capital in the South Sea Company and the rest in some other concerns even less reliable. I never had much faith in such ventures myself; but he was one of those who had, and their imminent failure fairly unmanned him. I thought he was one of the most thoroughly frightened men I had ever seen.'

'I have been told that Geoffrey Stannard felt a remarkably acute dread of death, even for a man of his years.'

'I think I sensed that myself. I thought it most unseemly in a Christian, though I declined to tell him so. But he did not seem to fear those diseases which are natural to old age, for he already suffered from arthritis and the gout. He also told me—in the strictest confidence, for he abhorred anyone's finding it out—that he was quite deaf in the left ear from a freakish accident in his boyhood: a devilish playmate had thrust a burning twig into his ear. No, what he held most in terror were those ailments that come without forecast and kill without discrimination.'

'You are thinking, then, of such impersonal infections as the plague?'

Ellis nodded energetically.

'The talk, if you remember, was all about how Marseilles and the rest of southern France had just been visited and how we were to be next. Everybody took on about it so—still do, some of them—but Stannard was wishing his heart in his boots, I could see that. As if the coming financial catastrophe where not enough for him.'

He paused for a moment and sipped at his coffee. He seemed to think that Man was expecting him to offer some substantial explanation or interpretation of Geoffrey Stannard's behaviour.

'I hardly knew him well, you understand, but I should

guess that what he feared most was what lay beyond his personal control. Stannard seemed to be one of those who felt the need to be master of every aspect of his destiny. I remember that in our conversation concerning the South Sea collapse he did not ask me what I thought was going to happen, but what could he do about it, what could be done to forestall or change the situation. He hated most, I think, his own helplessness. And that reached even to the rumours of the impending pestilence: "What can I do to save myself?" he would say; "Whither shall I fly?" I gathered that he had even curtailed his contacts with others, both in his business and in his home, for fear of something's being brought in unknown upon him. It was my impression — be it taken as it will — that he was a man prepared to do anything, commit almost any action whatsoever, to try to control his surroundings in order to ensure his private well-being.'

In the feeble light of the tavern, Man looked at his companion with the surprised respect which a middle-aged man sometimes feels for one young enough to be his son.

In his turn, Jack Ellis was probably wondering what had brought into the watchman's face a look that was part pride and part pain, as if his words had somehow awakened in the man certain precious, but unhappy, memories. He watched as Man appeared to retreat for a minute into reflection and then force himself back to the moment at hand.

'Did Mr Stannard, in his references to the fears of the plague in the present, ever include any allusion to the actual visitation in the past?'

'Now that you make mention of it, I believe he did say something of it. Yes, that's true, he must have been — what? — about my age, wouldn't you think, at the time. He did not speak much on it, mind you, only I recall that I myself entered it into the conversation. I think I must have wondered aloud what conditions must have been like during the worst months of sixteen-sixty-five and whether they compared in any way with those at large in France. Of course, I hesitated to ask him anything directly, in case he had suffered some personal loss that was yet too painful to think on. That is common, I think, among many.'

'And what did Mr Stannard say, do you remember?'

'He was—and there is, I'm afraid, no better word for it—somewhat evasive. That those days had left some mark in him was evident from his tone; other than that, I cannot recollect that I learned anything of a very private nature from him. He did mention—with a real sense of horror, as if it had all occurred but the day before—that he had been present at the start of it in Drury Lane and that he had been most fortunate to have escaped untouched. As something of an aside, he spoke out strongly against the failure of London's civic authorities to preserve the security of the people—adding that, if the public officials should prove negligent, then it becomes a private citizen to act in their stead. He said, I think, that it was not so much a duty as a right.'

By this time, Man felt that he had come to know Geoffrey Stannard so well that it would be difficult not to regard him as still living. The watchman could almost sense the presence of the old man, sharing the table with the two of them, sitting silently at Man's elbow. In his mind, he was aware of a natural confusion of the separate but successive time periods in Stannard's life.

Man leaned forward to make himself better heard above the crowd that was steadily growing more boisterous as the night lengthened.

'I have mentioned that Geoffrey Stannard died in the house in Drury Lane back into which his financial reversals had driven him. I might also add that he had since then acquired as a friend a young woman by the name of Nancy Flanner. Now, certain persons have suggested to me that this girl had some contacts among the garreteers of Grub Street. Does the name, then, mean anything to you?'

If Jack Ellis had noticed Man's use of the past tense, he gave no indication — or was too habitually diplomatic to let any show. Yet Man thought he did see something pass quickly behind the young man's look of polite interest. The watchman asked himself if it were mere distaste, or something more strong and personal. Ellis was young, but not especially striking in appearance.

'As it happens, Sir, I believe I do know of whom you speak. She has — how shall I word it? — neither the best nor the worst reputation among these men here. She is not offensive, but she is looked upon as one who keeps in with the lot rather as a low hang-on. She is said herself to have some aspirations towards writing, though I have never seen any samples of her work. It is, Sir, the fashion of our age — a pen in every hand — and one of which I, too, am guilty. Even our friend, Geoffrey Stannard, was rumoured to have lately planned to resort to some sort of writing as an attempt to alleviate his somewhat narrowed circumstances. Perhaps those volumes of memoirs, of which you have made mention, were intended by him for ultimate public consumption. But he never spoke the least of it to me.'

Man took a slow look round the room at the varied collection of faces, young and old. He had often heard these men referred to as eccentrics; yet they now seemed to him as quite common men, struggling and desperate, striving to endure by the only means available to them.

'Would you know if Miss Flanner had been seen more regularly in the company of any single gentleman — more, that is to say, than with any other?'

The face of Jack Ellis darkened with discomfort or, perhaps, with anger. He held his hands together before him on the table, picking with a fingernail at a small scratch on his hairless wrist.

'There is, I think I can say, one with whom she has been sometimes seen. I myself saw them once for a moment—not here, but at the Cock Tavern in Threadneedle Street, where I attend somewhat more frequently. An older man—much older than Miss Flanner certainly—small, a bit thin and sickly in appearance, poorly kept as a child I should imagine. Probably nearing sixty, yet I will say that he has on him an unusually boyish, timeless face. Deep, hollow voice that I have heard carry in a whisper quite across a room. Very dark eyes, but his vision is impaired. He reads with the paper held almost to arm's length.'

'Would you know the man's name?'

'That I would not, Sir. He is not known well among those who frequent these places. I gather he keeps himself something apart by his own choice. There are many who, for their work or for their shame, would wish to remain alone.'

Man felt in his pockets for the pipe he already knew was lying forgotten on the table at home.

'It may be, then, that you have heard some word spoken of the man's character or his circumstances.'

'Well, as to that, I have learned that he has spent many years at the lean trade of supplying anonymous material to whichever of the news-sheets happen to stand in need of it. As far as that lies, that is not extraordinary amongst us here. But he is said by some to work more in the way of repairing and editing than in creating.' This last observation seemed to give Ellis some private satisfaction. 'I would guess him to be as far from financial security as are the rest who run the newspapers—having, moreover, as I have heard, not only a wife to support, but also a fully grown son who has been paralysed and idiot since his youth. As to the man's character, I could not be a judge to that. What I cannot see, however, are what sort of dealings he could have with the Flanner girl. They could only prove to be another economic burden to him, not to mention the impropriety.'

Man studied the figure of Jack Ellis and concluded that the serious transition from boyhood to manhood lay still somewhere before him.

'Perhaps, in the light of his imperfect son, the man has yet some hopes of rectifying the situation.' Man felt awkward at the crudity of the implication.

The young face of Jack Ellis registered first surprise, then amusement.

'You may be allowing more to the father-son bond than is generally warranted. My own father, for one, was of a strange and meandering nature, an agile swordsman, but not much able to provide his children with the proper start in life. I myself was sent first, with a brother and two sisters, to a wretched day-school in Dogwell Court, Whitefriars, and then on to a marginally better one in Wine Office Court, Fleet Street. Not much of a precious beginning for a career which I hope will someday prove worthy.'

Later, as Ellis was preparing to go, Man asked him how he rated his own prospects in business, as compared to those he envisioned for himself in literature.

'As to the latter, I must confess that I consider myself to be without real talent. Yet as to the former, I hope it will appear no immodesty for me to say that I think I shall do very well indeed.'

'You have a secret plan, then?'

'The simplest, Sir. I plan merely to outlive everybody else.'

And as Man watched Jack Ellis thread his way through the crowd to the door, the older man thought that the younger might quite possibly succeed at that. And he wondered if Geoffrey Stannard had once had the same plan in mind and what he had had to do to try to make it become a reality.

Man had not had any news from Edward Scripture for a full week, and it had been more than two since he had delegated to his friend the task of identifying Nancy Flanner's 'older gentleman'. Scripture had as wide a range of contacts among the population of Grub Street as anyone; and besides, Man was now being kept especially harried by the marauding bands in St Giles. Scripture's early reports were far from encouraging: the girl and the unknown man had been seen frequently together by others, in addition to young Jack Ellis; the man was indeed a writer of sorts, but one who evidently valued his personal anonymity above all else; he was reputed by some to be a careless husband, yet an excessively doting father. No one could, or would, supply a name. It was almost as if the man had that kind of doleful, featureless personality that others automatically overlook or forget.

Yet Man could not allow himself to despair. He trusted that, eventually, Edward Scripture would return with some solid information. After all this work, Man hoped they were not all looking in the wrong directions.

Tonight, at least, he knew well enough what had to be done. Tonight was the time for what he chose to think of as indispensable sedentary research. Sometimes this involved concentrated reflection; sometimes he took advantage of a down-to-earth summation by his wife; and sometimes he was content with delving into London's nearly inexhaustible selection of newspapers and journals and books in the hopes of disclosing some particle of fact or opinion which would help him to see things more clearly.

He was seated now in his favourite chair near the fire, his blanket spread across his knees, a cup of gin and hot water nearby, one pipe burning at full force and a half-dozen others lying at his elbow, each already crammed with coarse tobacco. Between his outstretched feet lay Taylor Hoole's box of assorted specimens of plague literature. Round it, piled messily on the bare floor, were the books and pamphlets which Man had recently picked up from browsing among the bookstalls in the city. Leaning forward, he could smell the comfortable mustiness of the paper rising to mingle with the acrid fumes of his pipe and the sweet aftertaste of warm gin in his mouth. The warmth and ease which he was savouring were heightened by the rattle of the wet night-wind outside the house.

He liked his home, this room, at night; and he felt a certain regret that his work took him so much away from it and into the hard, freezing streets. From where he sat, he could just hear the even rise and fall of his wife's breathing, now alternating or synchronizing with the shallower breathing of the boy. Now that Toby was better and stronger and Sarah more rested, Man could turn his mind completely to the problem he had set himself.

There was an eerie contrast between the peacefulness of the house and the foreboding and panic described in the literature before him. With the smoke from his pipe curling lazily about his head and the muted crackling of the fire mimicking the sound of dry paper, he handled discoloured and frayed books that were over half a century old, smeared pamphlets containing no more than a few thousand words which had doubtless been privately printed for distribution among a limited circle of friends, and a few much more recently published volumes composed of better paper and more durable bindings. These last gave off the sharp odour of newness, and their innermost pages were cool to the touch.

Man sat back with three or four books in his lap and settled himself to begin reading. He had no intention of trying to read through each book in its entirety; he had always been a careful and perceptive reader, but a pain-fully slow one. Some of the books were quite long; and, with Nancy Flanner still missing, he had an uneasy feel-ing that he might not have much time left.

The major problem was that he did not have any firm idea of what he was searching for within these pages. He did not expect that any of the books could supply him with any definitive clue regarding the murder of Geoffrey Stannard. Some of them dealt exclusively with the last great plague in 1665; some with the contemporary fears of a new infection; others with the significant con-currence of the South Sea chaos and the impending doom of the returning plague. All that Man could realistically hope to find in such writings were some general insights into the mood of the times and possibly some detailed descriptions of some specific places and events. He thought he might be better able to understand the strange death of Stannard if he could share for a while the frame of mind of those people who had been involved in a situation that, in appearance, seemed unaccountably similar.

For he had felt all along that Stannard's murder had been labelled—consciously and deliberately or not—as something of an allusion, a reference to a time and an experience that somehow had a special meaning for the murderer. Man sensed that if he could only identify the importance of the allusion, then the identity and the purposes of the author would inevitably be revealed to him.

This was part of Man's method, because of which he was so often derided and misunderstood. To find the man who had killed Geoffrey Stannard required only the find-ing of the one man who must have killed him, who could not help but kill him. Some man who—due to the pressures of personality or circumstances—would not be able not to murder.

It was not long before the pages of the plague literature had Man enthralled. Sometimes tediously factual,
generally ill-written, the books still had the power to
evoke an atmosphere of disease and despair that affected
him even as he sat contented in the safety of his home.
One of the many lessons he had learned from his father
was that a man could suffer the loss of anything and still
endure—anything except the loss of hope. It was one of
the lessons which he had wished to pass on to his own son.
And here in these records—whether from the past or the
present—was the living death of a people, of a whole
society, without hope.

Man turned a page:

> In some houses carcases lay waiting for burial, and in
> others, persons in their last agonies; in one room might
> be heard dying groans, in another the ravings of a
> delirium, and not far off, relations and friends
> bewailing both their loss and the dismal prospect of
> their own sudden departure; death was the sure mid-
> wife to all children, and infants passed immediately
> from the womb to the grave. Who would not burst with
> grief to see the stock for a future generation hang upon
> the breasts of a dead mother? Or the marriage-bed
> changed the first night into a sepulchre, and the
> unhappy pair meet with death in their first embraces?

Man soon discovered that he was far more deeply
moved by the accounts dating from the last century than
by those more recent responses to the news of a fresh
pestilence in Marseilles. Whereas the contemporary
reports consisted mainly of a writer's pious exhortations to
a moral reform which would turn aside the judgement of
God, the historical chronicles depicted the pathetic
sufferings of a people confused and disheartened by the
inhuman raging of disease. The scenes of the city as it had

been some fourteen years before his birth sickened Man's heart:

> Now in some places, where the people did generally stay, not one house in an hundred but what is infected; and in many houses half the family is swept away; in some the whole, from the eldest to the youngest: few escape but with the death of one or two. Never did so many husbands and wives die together; never did so many parents carry their children with them to the grave, and go together into the same house under earth, who had lived together in the same house upon it. Now the nights are too short to bury the dead: the whole day, though at so great a length, is hardly sufficient to light the dead that fall thereon into their graves.

It would not do, thought Man, to let Sarah read such passages: it would only bring her old pain back again and make her all the more fearful for Toby.

As Man read on, extracting here and there an unemotional statistic from the bills of mortality or a horrifying portrait of the pest-house in the fields beyond Old Street, he gradually became aware of a peculiar pattern of markings in those books which belonged to Taylor Hoole. Most of the passages which his friend had especially noted had something to do with the watchmen who, in 1665, had been charged with guarding the shut-up houses. Man had heard before of the violence that had sometimes been done to these watchmen by the frantic inmates of the houses, but he was now surprised to learn how widespread the problem had been:

> There was likewise violence used with the watchmen, as was reported, in abundance of places; and I believe that from the beginning of the visitation to the end,

there was not less than eighteen or twenty of them killed, or so wounded as to be taken up for dead, which was supposed to be done by the people in the infected houses which were shut up, and where they attempted to come out, and were opposed . . . Nor do I remember that anybody was ever punished, at least to any considerable degree, for whatever was done to the watchmen that guarded their houses.

In this, the words 'eighteen or twenty' had been heavily underscored and a question-mark placed in the margin Even knowing Taylor Hoole as well as he thought he did, Man could not now answer for it.

The action of shutting-up infected houses proved to be a reference that recurred regularly throughout most of the books. And in a number of places the authors had regarded the legal closing of a house as something tantamount to murder:

One friend growing melancholy for another was one main cause of its going through a family, especially when they were shut up, which bred a sad apprehension and consternation on their spirits, *especially being shut up in dark cellars* . . . As soon as any house is infected, all the sound people should be had out of it, and not shut up therein to be murdered.

Man found himself shivering. Nothing that he read could disturb him as profoundly as this: a re-creation of such conditions in a community that had effectively legalized murder.

With the help of the gin and the baking fire, Man finally fell into that state of half-waking and half-drowsing in which the mind becomes absurdly sensitive and exaggerating. He found himself reading the same sentences over and over, as his head nodded over the opened book, without really comprehending the meaning. He was trying now to glance through a volume which had been published only last March; and certain parts of the text, like a conversation overheard, stood out in stark relief:

> We had at this time a great many frightful stories told us of nurses and watchmen who looked after the dying people . . . using them barbarously, starving them, smothering them . . . that is to say, murdering of them . . . and I have heard that three others, at several times, were excused for murders of that kind . . . some that killed them by giving them one thing, some another, and some starved them by giving them nothing at all . . . and deny me provisions for my money, is to say the town has a right to starve me to death, which cannot be true . . .

When Man awoke, stiff and chilled, the fire was out, and the books that had been in his lap lay scattered on the floor. A grey dawn was struggling through the frost-caked window. In the next room Toby was whimpering in his sleep, while Sarah was trying to soothe him with a melodic murmuring. The boards in the floor cracked with cold.

For a moment Man gazed stupidly about him, as though he were not sure where he was. He looked at the stone-cold idle back suspended over the dead fire and thought wistfully of a cup of strong coffee. His cramped body felt numb and old.

Without thinking, he bent forward and picked up one of the books he had just bought at a bookstall in the City. Listlessly, he remembered that the woman at the stall had told him that the book had come to her only a few days earlier. The title was barely distinguishable from most of the others: *A Journal of a Year of Death: Being a Local and Civic Relation of the Last Visitation in London of the*

Great Plague: Written by a Witness and Survivor. Nor did
the name of its author, 'Christopher Boyse', mean anything to Man.

Yet, with the manner of one who is still only semi-
conscious, he began to turn the pages, reading portions of
paragraphs or sentences at random. The writing, as well
as he could judge, was prosaic, with seemingly endless
series of mortality figures, quotations from Acts of
Parliament, and the prices of foodstuffs and coal. Man
could not help thinking vaguely that the style belonged
more to a tradesman—with something of the traditional
gift for tale-telling of that class of people—than to a
professional writer. There was overall a combination of
fact and story that made the historical accuracy of the
whole difficult to estimate.

Man's attention focused on the first few chapters, those
pages detailing the earliest suspicions among the people
of the plague's arrival. Not knowing why, he began to
read at a speed unusual for him, gradually becoming as
excited as he had been as a boy, participating in his first
official hue-and-cry. Now sitting alert in the lightening
room, he no longer felt the cold or his weariness. Now he
knew only the thrill one feels at encountering in print
what before had been only privately imagined.

The pages trembled slightly in Man's hands as he
turned them, and even Toby's crying out in fear did not
distract him.

By one of those coincidences which are so much more
easily accepted in life than in fiction, because they are
undeniable, Edward Scripture arrived with the name of
Nancy Flanner's Grub Street gentleman just as Man had
finished studying one particular chapter for the seventh
or eighth time. And by then he was sure that what he was
reading were the memoirs of Geoffrey Stannard; and the
name Christopher Boyse had become so inevitable and
obvious as to seem almost irrelevant.

CHAPTER 7

Therefore can no man pretend to know the
wretchedness of our days and the misery of our nights,
who has not himself heard the wailing of those distracted by pain or seen the wrought faces of those
others who are awaiting their own doom; none can
conceive of the fears and loathing which divides neighbour from neighbour. Now by day the commerce of the
street is all but suspended; I have seen the coal-
merchant trading at the door of some house, the
cleanest and the freshest in the street, and all the while
stand a good five paces back, and his face and mouth
hid behind the sleeve of his coat. It is this that must
seem the greatest fatality of the infection visiting our
town: not the suspicion between one man and the next,
which is any way a concern of the persons themselves,
not less than an half of them being solitary and mourn-
ful by nature; but it is the paralysing of the whole concourse in the city, the confusing effects on trade and
merchandising, the diminishing of traffick and of
transportation, that blights the life of the city in all
its parts and scenes. Even the young and strong are not
allowed the courage to pursue their futures, but
remain crouched in doorways or lie dreadful and
trembling in darkened rooms.

In every street, during the highest fever of the
plague, no more than an handful of the people are
escaped being touched: it may be but one man that
brings it in, and in a matter of days the effluvium is
handed from gossiping woman to woman, from servant
to shopkeeper, from the muddied child who makes his
wretched home in the road to the innocent passing

gentleman. None can know who is clean and who is not, for the earliest stages betray no symptoms or the victim himself is careless of the certain death he passes on by breath and by hand. The terror is that no man can be decided if another, talking with him of the weather in the street, is a new friend or a hidden executioner; or if, in the very congested air they share together, is not the invisible contagion attacking the both of them as they stand. The fear is, too, in the air, that most men are wont to harbour secretly within their own breasts. And that man that wills to survive must needs himself secure himself as best he might.

Christopher Boyse tenderly wiped the drool off the chin of his large, heavy-headed son, staring into his confused eyes and trying to quieten his wordless animal groanings. The boy seemed so especially upset today, even though he had been placed in his favourite spot near the window so that he could watch the late afternoon traffic passing on Shoe Lane. The father caressed him—the sweaty hair, the scarred flesh beneath the leather straps that bound him into the upright chair—and told him that he must try to keep silent, there were two important visitors in the parlour, he would come back to see him as soon as he could. The boy thrashed about spasmodically and moaned. He had the strength of a man, though without the control, and the father had to tighten the straps. He did so with the automatic gestures of years of experience and wondered—as he always did—how much the boy understood of what he said or did.

'I must beg your pardon, gentlemen. When my son is thus overwrought, his poor mother can do nothing with him. She is weak and nervous herself and only inflames him into further outbursts. He has become so accustomed to my being there beside him at this time of the day.'

Christopher Boyse settled his frail body on to the three-legged stool that he had taken in deference to his guests, who sat in the room's only chairs. He pulled the blanket up to his chest and slipped his arms through the two holes cut in the thin cloth.

One of the two watchmen — the younger, George Man, who appeared to Boyse to be the one in charge — gestured towards the next room and shook his head.

'We can only be sorry, Sir, to have to take you from one who needs you more. I hope we will not need to detain you long.'

Boyse noticed that his eyes were kind and pitying. Yet in the posture of his body and in the set of his mouth could be seen a grim determination.

The other man, Taylor Hoole, was nearer Boyse's own age and seemed to be more eager to please and reassure his host.

'I must congratulate you, Sir, before we open the business which has brought us here today, on the late publication of your book. It is, I understand, the first of your efforts to which you have assigned your proper name, and I think you may justly take great pride in it. I have myself made some study of such books as deal with the year of the Great Plague and its aftermath, and I feel yours to be one of the finest and most effective on the stalls. And, of course, the time for the book is ideal, the public's current fears running as they do.'

Boyse looked more closely at the monkish figure before him. Why, he asked himself, does he work so hard at trying to be amiable, as though he were inwardly trying to come to a painful decision?

The man beneath the blanket clasped his hands in his lap, entwining the fingers tightly together until they whitened.

'I must confess that I am not altogether unmindful of the present climate. We who write wish most to be read; and the more who feel inclined to read us, the more are we satisfied. I trust that I do not inadvertently fuel the public disquietude. I mean rather to show them how London once suffered greatly and still endured.'

The room was silent for a minute. Boyse cocked his head to one side, in a nervous gesture which he had never been able to break, to listen for his son's muted whimpering. Outside, the cold winds of November moved heavy grey clouds. It would snow soon.

The persistent watchman whom Boyse feared sat forward in his chair, fingering the pipe he had declined to light.

'How clearly, then, Sir, can you recall those days of the last visitation? If I judge your age correctly, you must have been but a small boy in sixteen-sixty-five.'

Christopher Boyse felt momentarily relieved.

'I do not know how well-acquainted you are, Sir, with the stratagems of the writing trade. A certain degree of licence is allowed in the re-creation of historical incidents. Direct narration of such events is often the best method of engaging the reader's attention. The same harmless imposture has been recently worked upon the public in another journal of that plague year — by one who is my own age and is, by his profession, a mere tradesman. My information comes from extensive research and from my conversations with some of those who still survive, not from the dim remembrances of my boyhood.'

I was living, in 1665, in that street which is called by the name of Drury Lane, a low enough district at that time and this, which was my hope to take myself out of by whatever means possible. With that end in mind, I had recently declined a prospect of marriage and elected to stop in the house of my parents, where I might better conserve my resources. My father was at this time a small dealer in used and worn clothing, which trade I from my boyhood found mean and insufficent; not only for the inglorious nature of the business itself and the debased qualities of the needful clientele: but also for the limited future it offers, with little hope of advancement or reward, a life of undistinguished want and a helpless death. My desiring to oppose my father's wishes occasioned not a few disputes amongst us: my father holding, with the brute obstinance of age, that a son's place is beside his father; while I say that the son has the right to select his own way, which must in any case outlast the days of the father. My own plan included, as I have before said, the taking of myself out of the hopeless neighbourhood in which the circumstances of my meagre birth had placed me; and make my way towards the City, where awaited finer opportunities of advancement; in brief, I meant to direct myself towards those offices where is the source of greater wealth and the mastery over the same. As a first step, I bethought myself of acquiring some property, land, or house, which I could buy at a low cost and later sell or rent out at a dear. I finally knew that such a course would leave me no time for a family of my own or even for leisure friends; yet, against the securing of my future, I counted these as but little. Also, I believed then, as I believe now, that I should so conduct myself in such a way that, should all my works come to fail, it should be the fault of those circumstances which lay anyhow outside my personal control.

'I should add that Miss Flanner has now been missing for some time, and her associations in the past have been such that we fear much for her fate.' George Man spread his hands in apology. 'If we have come to you, Sir, to ask if you might have had any news of the girl, it is simply because you were known to have been somewhat familiar with her—in connection with your trade, of course.'

Boyse had just returned from the kitchen with two dishes of transparent tea which his wife had brewed from last week's leaves. Boyse had not spoken to her, had had nothing to say, and she had only stared at him with the wounded expression of an animal that has suffered much and expects still to suffer more. As he had passed the doorway of the adjoining room, Boyse had been surprised and concerned not to hear the usual shifting of his son's chair. It was almost as if the boy were straining to listen, to overhear the fate of his father. The boy seemed worried. But that, Boyse told himself sadly, could not be possible.

It humiliated Christopher Boyse to have to offer his guests such a poor drink, but there had never been enough of anything in the house. He had hoped this book might change all that, but the payment had been far less than he had expected. He was too old, too powerless and unknown. He felt weak and sick.

And then the watchman had mentioned the name of Nancy Flanner with such abruptness and Boyse had been so overcome by a surge of nausea that he thought he would have to excuse himself again and retreat for a moment into the boy's room. He had fought to bring his racing mind under control.

A noise from the kitchen startled him. Was she listening, too?

'If you have learned, gentlemen, that I know Miss Flanner at all well, then I fear you have been badly informed. She is fond of keeping company with those who write, an association for which she is unhappily ill-suited. She has not had, you understand, the benefits of the sort of education that is such an enrichment of the young. She has youth, but little more. It is the tragedy of our times, Sir, to see so many being wasted in their early years for want of proper guidance.'

'And you have not seen or heard from her of late?' the

younger watchman persisted.

'Not for close on half a year, I should think, or some little less.'

'And had you then used to see her often?'

'No oftener, I imagine, than twice or thrice.'

'Where?'

'Quite by chance, in a tavern or coffee-house where such people as myself are wont to congregate.'

'Did she ever give you anything?'

'No.'

Christopher Boyse twitched his head again to one side, then stopped himself midway, remembering the curious look the watchman had given him the last time he had done so. He wondered suddenly if he had made the wrong response.

'That is to say, what could such a young girl possibly have that she could think I would want?'

Just as George Man was about to say something more, the other watchman interrupted. He spoke hurriedly, almost too loudly.

'You should have small chance, then, of having known any of Nancy Flanner's other friends or associates. She most probably had no cause to mention to you that she was at work at a chandler's in Drury Lane and that she knew well an old man who lived next door and is these two months dead. Geoffrey Stannard, his name was. But it appears to me that you keep yourself, Sir, in quite another circle. This man was, at one time, something of an important figure in the financial sectors of the city, although he had of late taken a turn downward.'

Boyse frowned as if in concentration.

'No, I am most sorry, but the name means nothing to me. And the little intercourse that Miss Flanner and I did hold centred solely upon books. For such a girl, she seemed to have a rather acute understanding of the state of writing in London today—I mean to say, the incertain monetary value of the written word and the desperation of those of us who attempt to sell it. And as you can see for yourselves, gentlemen—' he gestured wearily round the sparsely furnished, colourless room—'I have always been one of the least successful of vendors. I am neither well-known nor well-rewarded for such mechanical labours as I have had to do. I have worked for nearly forty years among the printers and sellers and publishers of this town, with neither the shelter of a patron nor the precedent of a notable lineage, and I am now something behind where I began. But to change now would require a change in my beginnings, which cannot be.'

He stopped and brought a hand to his chest to ease the tightness there that had been worrying him during the past year. He could not swallow and found it hard to draw a full breath.

The boy cried out almost savagely from the next room and Christopher Boyse rose slowly to his feet.

'It is unchristian of me to say so, but I am sometimes almost thankful for the impairment of my son's mind. It has spared him the pain of knowing what his father has become. You will excuse me, gentlemen.'

When he reached the doorway, he heard the voice of George Man behind him.

'What is the poor boy's name, Sir?'

Boyse was startled at the tenderness of the tone.

'Samuel. He is named after my own dear father.'

We had living with us at that time in the street an unfortunate family which was destined to play no small part in the tragedy of this year. The man, one G-- S--, was a carpenter by trade; but one who, as I thought, through some effeminate slackness in the application of his labours, which I add to his want of foresight and ambition in business, was doomed to a continual falling short of success. I remember that this man was much come into my father's shop, in need of some worn clothing or other; and that he always expended much time in the selecting of an article, time that would have been better spent over his workbench, tho' the item was no more than a bonnet for his child or a frayed handkerchief for his wife: and then, when time came to settle the account, to squander even more minutes in a debate over a penny, which my father would often concede him, tho' if I stood at the counter I would never give it him. He likewise made some repairs to my father's house, and would accept no more than credit or uneven trade, which I hold to be very remiss in him.

There was in the house with him his wife and son, the latter a boy of some five years or so. Of the woman, I cannot remark much, other than that she was thin in form and quiet in manner, and she took in washing from other houses in our street. Of the boy I can report more, from seeing him so much in the street or examining with longing some cap in our shop. Between father and son was a bond of the kind which I cannot help but call excessive, the boy devoting long hours of the day beside his father at the workbench that should have earned the family money in the streets by the running of errands or the holding of horses. How so may it be to the boy's credit in the learning of his father's trade, I who saw him working the tools in play can swear that the son never showed a fraction of the father's mechanical adroitness, whose talent itself was not in any case extensive enough. The boy was moreover sickly and ill-grown, short-sighted and hollow-chested, and was well-saved from the troubles soon to start, which would doubtless have early closed his young life.

I cannot too much animadvert upon this discomforting propensity among parents to so much exert their attentions upon a mere child. In this instance, as this was the sole issue of the marriage, some will say such conduct may be apprehensible; yet even in this, it is my thought that such doting transcends beyond all reasonable measure.

It is not to be thought that I myself had as much direct concourse with this family as may be supposed from my foregoing words, which ran mainly to those exchanges which I have before noted and to whatever hazardous conjectures I may have formed upon observation; but I elaborate at such length by reason of the central rôle which the house, in especial the father, was soon to enact in the lives of myself, of the other citizens in the street, and of all of London. That a single individual could have such a profound effect upon such a large body of people, and that a most horrid one, is now scarcely to be believed: yet the year of which I write was such a one of wonders unnatural and demented that exhausts the powers of description.

It was, I think, some time in the earliest months of that year that I first began to mark an oddness in the appearance and behaviour of the man S-- that had before seemed to me as steady and robust as any. In the first, this consisted of no more than the man's increased absence from the street, in his almost always staying within doors, tho' he had ever been sedentary in his habits, owing to his trade, but which was of a sudden aggravated to a remarkable degree. Whole days passed without a sighting of him or even an opening of the door for airing. He was accustomed, as are the most of us, to stopping in at a shop of an evening for a cup or a dish: but even that was now forgone and ignored. Then, after the space of a week or more, I spied him once more in the street with a load of wood. I stopped him and questioned him about him keeping himself indoors; and the only answer he could

make me was, I thought, a feeble one; viz., that he was
much taken with the head-ache and back-pain. Not
three days after, I watched him from my window,
passing up the street, his skin pallid and a cap tied
firmly to his head and a heavy band of cloths wound
round his neck. This, at a time when the weather was
memorably clement for the season. It was this
appearance of the man thus that first brought me to
consider that he might be seriously ill; and, next, that I
myself, from talking with him in the close air of the
lane, might well be infected, should he prove to suffer
from some noxious contagion. Within an hour of my
thinking thus, I began to take notice of a growing lump
behind my right ear, and was made much afraid that I
might lose all my hearing in that one, too; tho' this
time not by childhood accident, but by the reckless
coming abroad of our heedless neighbour. We had all
of us heard tales of such pestilence as the plague,
primarily in Holland, and of the impersonal doom it
carried, and I feared that soon such a thing might be
brought amongst us that no man had the power to
withstand or control, and I must see an end to all my
programme for my future.

I therefore went out among my other neighbours,
informing them of my dread, and exhorting them to
precipitate action. In such examples, I knew, the loss
of but a day could equal the loss of a life. The other inhabitants of the street I found at first to be quiescent
and disinclined to move, as were the civic officials to
whom I sued for security. I bethought myself then that
in such moments it falls upon the individual as a
mortal right to create a vigilance where he finds none.
Finally, after much visiting of homes and energetic
argumentation, I had the majority of the people
behind me in my efforts to contain the infection and
preserve those of us who were yet whole.

At this same time, unbeknownst to me, the man himself must have somehow learned of what went forward; and, instead of openly confronting me with the truth of the matter, did darkly send forth both wife and child to a ship that a friend of his kept upon the river. Why he himself did not remove with them I could not guess; tho' some averred it to be his fear that some bad report would follow them, if he carried himself along with them: tho' I contended that it was as good as a confession from the man himself, that he knew himself to be truly touched with the plague, and was desirous of saving his own. I was later informed that wife and boy were departed with that same Heath family, which lived in the house next theirs.

He could not account for it. The watchman named Hoole had been talking rather casually about some family of his acquaintance who lived nearby in the same lane. The other watchman had stood up and wandered idly over to the half-dead fire, readying his pipe in his hand. He had before promised not to smoke, for fear of fouling the air in the boy's room, though Boyse could sense that the man was yearning to light the tobacco he kept tamping down into the bowl of his cold pipe.

Then, without knowing what was happening, Boyse had heard a quick sharp crackling thrust very close to his head and had instinctively jerked his body to the right. It was the watchman, holding forward a still-burning stick from the fire and mumbling his apologies. For a moment, Boyse had the thought that the man was somehow lunatic and intent upon setting his host's head on fire or attacking him from behind. It had shaken Boyse badly; his nerves were already quite on edge from this strange, indirect interrogation.

George Man was back in his chair now, seemingly content to sit with his hands crossed in his lap and to stare at some point on the bare wall behind Boyse. Taylor Hoole sat fidgeting in his own chair, and once or twice Boyse could hear him sigh deeply.

Boyse himself felt that he could hardly breathe. The habit he had developed during the past few months of moving a closed hand before his mouth, as if he were trying to force more air into his lungs, now bothered him almost ceaselessly. He wanted desperately for this interview to be over, even if it meant the worst.

George Man still avoided looking directly into Boyse's face.

'Your own family comes from Drury Lane, as I understand it.'

'What makes you say that, Sir?'

The watchman's eyebrows rose.

'Why, I believe, Sir, it is what you yourself wrote.'

They were back to the book.

'Again, you must make some allowance for the writer's freedom with the literal truth. My family came from quite near that area, and I can remember passing often through Drury Lane in my youth. The character of the street made it such that my fearful mother forbade my entering it; and, as with all children, the restriction only made me wish to visit there all the more.'

Behind him, Boyse could hear that his wife had now moved into his son's room. It irked him; he had told her often enough that the boy did not feel at his ease with her.

'Did you have any particular playmates there?'

'It was all so long ago, and I left that district when I was yet a very small boy, so you cannot expect me to remember much.' Boyse rubbed his forehead, trying to still the shaking of his hand. 'I was, in any case, a solitary child, not much given to the street-games of the other boys. I had then as few friends as I have now.'

This sounded more pathetic than he had intended. He did not really feel that he needed any other person's company. He had his son and his work: at his age, what more could he want?

'That section, then, in the early pages of your book—that detailing the first suspicion of the plague in Drury Lane—is that, too, mainly fictional, or is it founded more securely upon fact? It seems to me that I have heard the old speak of the infection's beginning in that very street.'

'That is much said, it is true,' Taylor Hoole broke in, 'but more reliable informants have told me that the first true manifestation occurred at the upper end of Drury Lane—more specifically, in Long Acre—and that the initial victims were said to be Frenchmen. Of course, before the present resurgence of fear and so many years after the event, 'twas something of a claim of importance to argue that the past plague began in one's own street or in that of one's grandmother. People are most eager to participate in a general disaster, once the doom of it is no longer at their doors.'

'You have said well, Sir,' spoke Boyse with an enthusiasm which surprised even him. 'I can recall my own poor mother's saying that to be so close and yet to have escaped unharmed not only demonstrated the Creator's special care for us, but also made of us members of a select group of survivors which would be wondered at in later years. I cannot say that I myself much feel the truth of that in my own life, but certainly there must be many who do. Nearer our own time, we have those in London who suffered grave experiences during the Great Storm of seventeen-three and never weary of speaking of it yet.'

Christopher Boyse could not understand why, when he had said this, George Man grew suddenly moody and thoughtful. He seemed to be remembering something and, at the same time, trying to comprehend the meaning of what he remembered.

After a moment, the watchman trained his look upon Boyse.

'Whatever the historical truth of the matter may be, I ask you again, Sir, of the accuracy of your own rendition of the events in Drury Lane. Surely such a notorious example must have made some deep impression even in a boy of few years.'

The room was getting darker; but Boyse could not decide if this were due to the hour or to the small windows of the house and the narrow lane outside. He did not know the time.

'It is true that such an incident as is described in those pages did occur in that street at that time; but my memory of it is shadowy at best, and I have had to supplement it with my own fancy. I believe the bare outline of events is particular enough, though some of the characterization may be of my private design. It signifies nothing that the specific be at fault, if the general be truthful.'

'It is yet possible, then, that—as a boy yourself—you may have known the boy who, with his mother, deserted and abandoned the ailing father to his fate. Or perhaps one of your brothers or sisters.'

Boyse felt the blood rush suddenly into his face, and he tottered slightly on his stool. His voice sounded brittle in his ears.

'Brothers and sisters I have, and had, none. And as I recall the incident, both in the book and in my memory, the boy and mother neither deserted nor abandoned the poor man, but were sent away at his frantic bidding to their salvation. Think you it humanly possible, Sir, that any wife or any child should willingly forsake such a selfless man, unless they were forced against their own desires to do so?' He tried to check his anger. 'You must, I am afraid, know pitiably little of that inseverable and eternal bond which exists between father and son.'

'Eternal . . . yes . . . I know.' The watchman became thoughtful again and his manner softened. Taylor Hoole moved uneasily in his chair. 'Perhaps,' George Man went on slowly, 'we may conjecture from this that the man did indeed carry the pestilence, and knew it, and therefore acted as he did to save his family from certain infection.'

Boyse half-rose from his seat. His entire body became taut.

'That I shall never, never believe, Sir! If I spoke before of their salvation, I meant it to refer to their escape from the unjust persecution of their ignorant neighbours. There was no proof, never any proof whatsoever, that the man did in fact suffer from the plague.'

No one said anything. Boyse realized with a sickened feeling that he should not have spoken out as he did, nor so strongly. He knew that he had now directly contradicted what he himself was supposed to have written. And the two watchmen continued to look at him in silence.

Boyse pulled the blanket farther up his chest. He wanted only to be alone in the next room, talking to his son. He felt impossibly old.

'May I now ask you, Sir, the reason for such questions concerning the distant past, and what relation they may have to the stated purpose of your coming to see me today—the abrupt disappearance of this girl, Nancy Flanner. I fail to see the slightest connection.'

It was a feeble effort, but it was as much as Boyse thought he was capable of. He looked first towards the older watchman, who looked away, and then at the other. George Man was still toying with his idle pipe, his lips pursed and his forehead lined, his eyes searching for something on the uneven floor. He seemed not to have heard what Boyse had said, or not to have listened.

From the next room came the sounds of a minor struggle. Boyse knew that his wife was trying, unsuccessfully, to get the boy to eat.

At last, the watchman raised his head and looked across at Boyse and said reluctantly:

'I should like to ask you, Sir, something about your father.'

We commenced our labours that very night of the meeting, at some hours past midnight, when the street was empty of citizens and the watchman was passed; the night was clouded and without stars, which was to serve our purposes; as we were not very desirous of making ourselves known, so as not to fright whichever innocent neighbour as might by accident emerge from his house or window. We had also taken the needful precaution of obscuring our heads and faces in dark cloaking hoods, with holes cut into them for the eyes. There were of us, as well as I can remember, a dozen or more: all men who lived, as did I, with their separate families in the street; and who were assured, at my urgings, as I have before related, that their safety and the preservation of their homes was in peril. The night was cold; and some, to arm themselves against the chill or, as I thought, against the timidity of their own natures, had taken strong drink and even carried it in the street with them; tho' I, because I remained sure in our designs, disdained it; and I continued to talk strongly against those who did not, and who were made thus heedless in their walking and their actions.

One man amongst us, he who knew the object of our plans better than the rest and who, before the present scare, had been often in his home; joining the family at table or the father at the childish games he was used to play with his son: a rashness which he, I mean the man who made one of our number, now much repented, calling the man devilish and a murtherer of his neighbours; he, I say, was elected to knock the door and halloa the man up and out, tho' he steadfastly refused to pass the threshold, as did all others of our company. It was I who had to stand forward as he who would enter the house and subdue the plague-carrier; for which purpose I had before supplied myself with a cloth for the man's mouth, to silence his cries, and a cord for his limbs, if he should choose to struggle.

The man having been shouted up and the door unbarred, I made an entrance, under the pretext of having some urgent news of his wife and son, all the while taking care to avert my face from his, and to maintain some good distance between us. As I looked upon him, in the light of his night-candle, he looked to be even more wan and strengthless than before; and I was the more assured of his mortal condition and of the need for making all haste. In a moment he was turned away from me, I availed myself of a heavy tool which was lying carelessly about, which was always the habit of the man, he being most irregular in his labours, and struck him full upon the rear of the head. In my ardour, I may have acted with somewhat more force than I intended, but the effect was the same; viz., I quickly gagged and bound him, collected some of his wood and tools, and made my exit. I left him in the kitchen, to where he had led me for a cup.

Outside, I breathed easier the clean night-air; and as one we boarded up the door and windows, a ladder having been secured in my absence, and affixed a notice of quarantine on the door. In three weeks or more, when the plague was manifested fully upon us, the house was opened by certain officials of the parish, and the body removed to a common grave: the death being entered upon the bills of mortality as an incertain case; whereas, tho' the man had not the tokens of the plague upon him, yet this in itself signified little, as he evidenced the contortions and the fearfulness of expression characteristic of that infection. As for the wife and the boy, they never returned, even after the close of this terrible year; whether because they dreaded the opprobrium of the street or because another had already expressed his interest in the house, I was never able to determine.

In later and more settled times, some observers may fault us for the precipitancy of our acts, saying that such decisions and such executions lay in the hands of the lawful officers of the town; yet our time was much troubled and the chief officers much confused and lax: and, in such extremes, it behooves the private individual, with the vocal or silent acquiescence of the neighbourhood, which last we had, to move against any visible or hidden threat to the conservation of the peace and strength of the society. And though none of us stepped forward at the time to own our actions, the temper of the times being feverish and severe, and the probability of us being ourselves accused of being carriers of the contagion, myself for one having been within the man's house with him; yet in these days, when the people are more certain of which due preparations they should effect against a new visitation, it is my thought that most must condone and understand that we then had none other choice but to declare, among the leading citizens of the street, the man's life to be illegal.

If only the watchman had given him more time to think, to decide how much of the truth was safe to tell, to choose which answer would sound the most innocent and believable. He had never been able to think clearly or well under pressure. He had simply needed more time, time to try to understand the special significance of each question and to formulate a satisfying response.

And there had been so many questions. What street had he lived in, after he had left the area of Drury Lane?

Did his mother ever work at anything? Was his son's impairment possibly derived from some illness in his own parents? When did his mother die, and of what and where? Could he remember having spent any time on a ship as a boy? Could he work well with his hands? Had he ever heard the name Emeny? And dozens more, each more probing than the last.

And then the questions about his father. How could he tell the truth? And yet how could he not be true to the memory of the man who, after a period of over half a century, still meant so much to him? Christopher Boyse had spent almost all his childhood, and the whole of his adult life, thinking about and missing his lost father. He had known him for such a brief time, yet the memories were as strong and clear as if he had been beside him every day of his life. How could he express his feelings about the man who, for him, had never really died?

He had said as much as he thought he safely could and invented the rest. Yes, in a way his father had worked in wood, but only as a painter of furnishings. Of course he had been very close to him; but what boy is not? That a father should leave off his work for a few hours in a day to play with his son may not be as common amongst us as it ought; but how is it unique? Surely the watchman's own father must have done much the same.

Boyse had continued to feel more and more weary and disorientated. It had become increasingly difficult for him to distinguish past from present, fiction from truth. As the afternoon had given way to night, he had begun to sense that he was nearing the end of a very long process before he had had the time to prepare himself for it.

And then the watchman had steered the conversation towards more general terms, speaking of the father-son relationship both in the present and the past, and how so little had really changed. It was at this moment that Boyse had started to let himself feel more relaxed and secure. Such impersonal topics, he thought, could only be less threatening to him. The further they digressed from his own life's story, the story contained in the book, the better it would be for him and for his son. Boyse did not care to think of the boy's being alone without him. So with a look of interest and an occasional nod of the head, he had encouraged the watchman in his harmless monologue.

But now, just as Boyse had begun to feel that the interview was drawing to an end, the watchman was changing his theme once again. Now, seeming to be caught up in his own words, he was setting forth such outrageous and eccentric theories that Boyse felt more confused than ever.

'Yet I was thinking,' the watchman droned on in an even tone, 'but the other day, that the present fashion among the young to criticize and disdain their parents — which the parents themselves much detest — is not really the crime it may appear to be, but a natural consequence of the children's coming of age. What more could we want for them, but a truly independent turn of mind and a will to live their own lives as they wish? I think it most easy for a child to forget his parents, but far more difficult to make the parents forget about him. I wonder if the most perfect love may not be that which knows no affection. There is my good friend Isaac Hervey, now. I would call the relationship which he and his father enjoy an estimable one. And yet they have been known to pass each other in the street with absolutely no sign of recognition between them and with neither rancour nor goodwill in their hearts. This comes, I would suggest, from their being two separate and complete individuals. And this is something which I feel we all must esteem and desire.'

Boyse wondered if the man actually believed in such wildly absurd ideas, or if he were speaking deliberate nonsense merely to provoke him. And, sitting there before the calm figure of the watchman, Boyse could feel himself becoming, almost against his will, gradually incensed, as though he were being personally offended. His breathing quickened and his head ached, until he knew that he must speak out.

'Sir, I do not know from what you derive such outlandish opinions; but it cannot be from real human experience, of that I am certain. A man without a son is but half a man, and a boy without a father faces a vacant future. It is not so simple a thing as a name and a lineage, although these are to be considered; nor is the relationship merely that of teacher and student or master and servant. There is more, much more. There is the companionship between them, so that neither needs to feel alone in this world. There is that which each of them sees in the other, so that neither should think himself too different from his kind. There is, too, something binding them together which cannot be expressed in words — an instinct that they have both sprung from the same root. A man who has lost his son is pitiful indeed, for he has lost his reason to go on. And a son who has lost his father is himself lost in life.'

Boyse paused to steady his thoughts. He had meant to continue, but was suddenly distracted by the other watchman, Taylor Hoole. The man was sitting forward in his chair, tensed with emotion, and was beginning to speak. What surprised Boyse most was that the man was not looking at him, but at his fellow watchman; and he spoke directly to him, as if Boyse were no longer in the room. To Boyse, his voice sounded almost imploring.

'I can feel that, Sir, what this man has said. There is no other tragedy so moving and significant as the death of the father. Beside it, all other losses pale, even the death of mother or wife. It is a deprivation from which no man can ever recover.'

The other watchman frowned at him.

'And may I ask what special intelligence entitles you to speak so, Mr Hoole?'

'It is because I myself have suffered the same lot as have so many others. My own father—a watchman like ourselves, Sir—was one of those officers who fell beneath the inhuman abuse of his fellow citizens during that terrible year of which Mr Boyse has written. He was one who had been set to guard a house of plague victims; and they, in their frenzy to escape and quit the town, overpowered him and beat him to death. I was but a week old when they brought him home on a board; but I continued to feel my mother's loneliness and my own misery well into manhood. It dissuaded me for long from turning to the work which I now follow. The felons were never even sought after for their crime—a crime which, in its effect, destroyed more lives than one.'

'And a crime which, before all others, must not go unanswered.' Boyse could no longer control himself. His hands shook violently. 'We punish the thief and the seducer, but who is left to punish those who have stolen a child's blood and blighted his innocence? What is the passing of time to the completion of justice? What is needed is payment—payment for a lifetime of yearning—payment in kind!'

Boyse slumped over, exhausted, on his stool. He could not stop the twitching of his head. The room was silent, except for the gurgling sound George Man made on the pipe which he was now lighting at the fire.

The watchman returned to his chair. He looked at Boyse with a face that seemed almost inhuman in its total lack of expression. Boyse thought of cold, dead ashes.

'And would you now tell us, Mr Boyse, exactly when and under what circumstances your father met his death?'

Boyse sat still for a moment; then he rose slowly to his

feet, glanced blankly at the two watchmen, and turned to walk towards the doorway leading into his son's room.

The boy was still at the window, now opaque with darkness. The mother had left a candle burning on the floor. A plate of uneaten bread and a cup of milk lay on a small table.

Boyse knelt in front of his son, holding his hands over the boy's. He felt calmer now. He looked into the boy's empty face and wished he had the time to say everything he wanted to say. Now, it did not seem to matter much, if his son could not understand him.

'A while ago I left you, Samuel, with your mother, because I had something very important which I had to do. I told you then, remember? And I did come back.' He brushed the hair back from the forehead. His hand came to rest on the boy's neck. 'Now, I may have to go away again for a little time, and I want you to remember that I will come back again. Do not forget. I will be with you again.'

He kissed his son full upon the eyes and tasted tears.

When Christopher Boyse stepped back into the parlour, he saw Taylor Hoole sitting with his fingers pressed hard against his eyes. The other watchman was walking towards Boyse. He was already wearing his greatcoat.

CHAPTER 8

'What kind of man is he?'

They were seated before the fire. As always, Sarah had her sewing and Man had his pipe. The night was cold and stormy. Snow was piled up thickly at the lower corners of the window, and stars of frost patterned the glass. Toby had been asleep for hours.

Man took a generous drink of his hot gin.

'An incomplete man, I should call him. Strengthless, without confidence, out of place even in his own home; he suggests a youthfulness that is neither innocent nor hopeful, but simply immature. He has the experience without the understanding. In a man of his years, that is tragic.'

'Has he yet confessed to anything?'

'Nothing. But he is a man not so much without guile as without energy. He is wholly dispirited, as if a part of him had been cut off in boyhood and had never grown back. He has never been able to succeed at any thing in his life, not even murder.'

'Because you found him out, Sir.'

Man stared hard at the glowing sphere of fire in the bowl of his pipe.

'Not that only, Madam. I feel that he still believes the murder of Geoffrey Stannard was just and necessary, as I believe it to have been inevitable. Yet the death of the man who killed his father has brought him no peace, nor has it been able to make his life any more meaningful. If anything, it made his life more empty, for it deprived him of his hatred.'

'So he put an end to Mr Stannard in that horrible manner to avenge his father.' She shivered and bent more earnestly over her sewing.

'But revenge is not the best word for it. Rather "repayment" — as he himself said, "payment in kind." The way in which he killed Stannard had been decided for him some fifty-seven years earlier. I will tell you something further, Mrs Man. I have reason to suspect, as I may have suggested to you some weeks ago, that Boyse stayed in the shut-up house for part or all of the time in which it took Stannard to starve to death.'

'The remains of candles in the garret?'

'And something which Mr Caddick intimated about

Nancy Flanner's continuing to visit the house during the month in which Stannard himself was supposed to be away. Why else, but to bring in secret to Boyse sustenance of one kind or another?' Man knew the delicate nature of his wife, and he did not care to tell her all of his suspicions. 'Think on it, Sarah. Christopher Boyse spent all of that time in that small room, possibly reading and re-reading the volumes of Stannard's memoirs or possibly just — listening.'

'My Lord, Mr Man, no!' She stopped her sewing. The wind knocked at the window, throwing against it frozen snow that sounded like fine grains of sand.

'He had to be there, had to witness everything to the end. I do not pretend to a full understanding of any man's heart; but I think that Boyse had always felt himself somehow to blame for his father's death, for having left him there to die alone. He was but a boy of five at the time, you will remember. Children often cannot comprehend their own guiltless helplessness. Throughout his life, a part of Christopher Boyse had, I think, always felt that he should have been there, there in the boarded-up house beside his father. Yet I do not believe that even he himself knew why he felt compelled to stay and listen to Stannard die.'

Sarah Man pulled her shawl more snugly about her shoulders.

'It is a nightmare scene which I beg you, Sir, not to bring before me again.'

Her husband blew the moisture out of his pipe, filling the air above his head with spiralling smoke.

'But why,' his wife resumed, 'did the poor man wait until now to commit the deed? Is it because there is this year a return of the people's fears of the plague? But how could he have foreseen that?'

Man patiently shook his head.

'The times, of course, gave him a perfect context for

the manner in which he carried out the murder. Some argue still that the death of Geoffrey Stannard is related to the pestilence. And, in its own way, it is.' He sat forward and counted off on the fingers of his left hand with the stem of his pipe. 'It was a sequence which, once set in motion, had to run on to its natural end. Look you: the collapse of the South Sea Company gives Stannard the need to repair his losses with a new venture, and the forecast reawakening of the plague—and the spate of popular books which it released—gives him the means by which he might once again achieve success. So he writes his memoirs, a record of one who was present at the start of the Great Plague. And then Christopher Boyse, a writer and editor by profession, reads the volumes and discovers, for the first time, the truth about the death of his father and the man who was most culpable in it. I am convinced that, before the autumn of this year, Boyse knew nothing of the truth. He had been so young at the time of his father's death, and I would imagine that his mother was too kind of a woman to tell him all.'

'But how could he have met with the writings? Not by mere chance, I should think.'

'You are forgetting, Madam,' said Man, 'the intervention of young Nancy Flanner. The particulars of that connection we may never decide, if Boyse should never confess nor the girl ever be found. I would guess that she had known Boyse, slightly or well, for some months; and that, in her talks with Stannard, the old man might have told her of, or even read her parts of, his memoirs and may even have mentioned the name of Samuel Boyse. Then Miss Flanner—who, I am afraid to say, was rather too well-accustomed to judging all things according to the amount of money they would bring her at market— estimated that such a book might be of great interest to Boyse, who would probably reward her efforts more handsomely than the niggardly Stannard. It is most likely that, some time in the month of August, she took at least the first volume of Stannard's writings, for a night or for a few hours only, and brought it to show to Boyse. And, after reading those early pages dealing with his father, Boyse's course was set.'

Sarah wagged her head and fetched a long, deep sigh. Man recognized that gesture. It was his wife's way of saying that she knew such people did exist, but that it taxed her poor imagination to believe it.

Suddenly she remembered something.

'Was it not, Mr Man, in the final week of October that you came in with the dawn, fairly crowing that you had succeeded in tracing the memoirs to Nancy's hands? Yet I recall your remarking that she had offered the papers to some receiver. Now, why would Boyse have let her do that?'

Man scowled in self-reproach.

'If I had thought rightly at the time, Madam, and gone first to see the girl instead of Mr Wild, Nancy Flanner might yet be alive today. Yes,' he hurried on, seeing his wife's shock, 'I do not doubt that she has been for these months beyond our aid. But to answer your question: he did not. It is my notion that the girl somehow took the volumes from Boyse's house while he was out — an easy enough chore for one of her experience — in the hopes of being able to procure a higher price for them for herself. It may be that she had come to doubt the steadiness of Mr Boyse or had regrets, after my talk with her, about her part in such a grave crime. Whatever the case, in a few days Boyse must have surmised her defection, demanded that the writings be returned to him, and subsequently repaid her as he had Stannard. This seems to me to be approximately what must have occurred, considering the characters of the two persons involved.'

Man again refrained from adding any other interpretations of the exact nature of the relationship between

Flanner and Boyse and how the man, besides feeling betrayed, may well have felt rejected.

His wife, however, seemed reluctant to admit such cruelty in the pathetic figure of Christopher Boyse.

'I should think your Mr Wild might be the more likely to have punished the girl for what he would think was her treachery towards him. That is in his style.'

'That, too, is not impossible.' Man had winced at his wife's expression. He knew that she did not approve of his casual acceptance of some of London's most infamous and vicious felons. 'That man merits close watching in the years ahead. Howsoever it may have happened, it is sad that the girl was so unfortunate and careless in her choice of companions.' He paused for a lengthy sip from his drink. 'Oh, and have I mentioned that these same volumes of manuscript writings of which we speak have been discovered in the house of Christopher Boyse? They are not, of course, in his hand.'

She had turned her head towards the bedroom door-way to listen to the boy tossing in his sleep. Now she looked across at her husband with affectionate exasperation.

'This is another thing, Sir, that I must ask you to explain to me. You know that I am but a simple woman, with hardly a whole thought in my head from one day to the next. Now, I am all confusion. I have read, and had read to me, these parts from this book that you have marked out. And I understand that the girl, Nancy Flanner, may have viewed the papers merely as something she could exchange for money. Yet is that why Mr Boyse wished to publish them, solely for gain? And why under his own name? And how were you, Sir, so assured that the book was really Stannard's work and not Boyse's?'

Man sat back, puffing vigorously on his pipe. He did not mind discussing his ideas at length with his wife; his work took him so much away from her that he thought she deserved as complete an explanation as he had to offer.

'You, too, Madam, would have been as certain as I, had you had the opportunity of meeting Christopher Boyse. As I have said, he is a weak and unsettled man, too much taken up with the tragedy of his childhood and with the insignificance of his adult life. Yet, with all this, he seems to be neither entirely concerned with himself nor meanly intent upon amassing a personal fortune for his sole benefit. Now, on the other side of it, the man who records his recollections within the pages of this book is—as Stannard himself was reputed to have been, by all who knew him—a grasping, small, unconscious sort of man who would stay at no extreme to see himself secure and well-advanced. The two men could not be further apart.'

'Then why could Mr Boyse not have written in the guise of another? That is often done these times, is it not?'

'Let me tell you,' Man went on eagerly, 'what first suggested to me that the book which has been published as the work of Mr Boyse is in fact the personal journal of Geoffrey Stannard. In sixteen-sixty-five, in Drury Lane, there lived a man who—by reason of an accident suffered in his boyhood—was totally without hearing in his left ear. That man was Geoffrey Stannard. He was a proud man, and he was careful not to advertise his infirmity. He, of course, knew of it. A young scrivener by the name of Jack Ellis knew, because Stannard himself had told him a few years ago. I knew, because Jack Ellis told me. But how, wife, how could Boyse have known of it? Yet there it stands in the book. He claims never to have met the old man—and I believe he never did. Until, that is, the day he entered the house that was his as a boy, to murder and to rob.'

Sarah Man studied her husband with admiration. She took as much pride in his understanding of people and their actions, as she did in his essential goodness. They had known each other now for nineteen years; and, during that time, she had watched him struggle again and again to find out the truth of some human problem. She had congratulated him when he succeeded; she had comforted him when he failed: but she had always admired him.

'I should think, Sir, it had been better to revise the book, especially those parts which touch upon Mr Boyse's own past, in an attempt to disguise what ought not to be revealed.'

'Boyse may have had neither the time nor the talent to do so. He was currently at work upon a large project for one of the booksellers, and he was already far past the date which had been prescribed for its completion. He did, however, of necessity alter the initials of his father. I have myself examined the manuscript page: the letters "S-- B--" have been crossed through and the letters "G-- S--" supplied in their stead. The original must have given Boyse the final proof that the man put to death in Drury Lane in sixteen-sixty-five was indeed none other than his father. I had suspected such a change, when I first read the printed book. Stannard would hardly have wanted to use his own initials, and for Boyse to alter them to Stannard's must have seemed to him a satisfying inverse justice. The name of Heath—which he may have remembered from his childhood—he did not bother to disguise, probably because he could not imagine anyone of that name still surviving from so long ago. Yet Mother Emeny lives on.'

Sarah gestured with her needle.

'I can see that he would want the true story of his dear father told and that he might even take some pride and solace in pretending to be its teller. Yet Mr Boyse himself, in presenting the book as his own, must have felt himself to be acting the part of his own father's murderer!'

Man took some moments to reply, reflecting gravely

upon the meaning of what he was to say.

'Do you not understand, Mrs Man, that this is how he must have inwardly felt since his earliest years? A small child is sent away from the father he adores; the father dies; the child thinks that if he had only been there with the man, perhaps he could have fought off the murderer with his wooden sword, or made his father tiny and hidden him in the corner behind his toys, or the two of them would only have had to close their eyes and become invisible. It is how a child thinks—and how a man thinks, if he has never been able to leave his childhood behind him. Why else would the adult Christopher Boyse, having shut up the house for the second time, have thought to call himself Stannard's son? Why else would he have chosen to remain in the house for such a long while, listening to the old man's writhings and groanings of mortal starvation? Boyse is not a strong man, emotionally. I think that, hidden alone up in that darkened garret, he might well have imagined that the far-off death-agonies of the man downstairs were those of his own father. Boyse was finally doing what he believed he should have done fifty-seven years before.'

They sat in silence, while the snow continued to cake the window. Man felt a twinge of stinging hurt in his wounded shoulder. He thought it had been perfectly healed by now.

'Well,' said Sarah with finality, 'it has been a long work for you, Sir, coming to find Mr Boyse.'

Man snorted in disgust.

'And if it had not been for my own backwardness of mind, I could have come to him much sooner. Old Mother Emeny told me more than either of us knew. Can you guess it, wife? What I heard as "poor boys, poor boys"—thinking there had been more than the one child in sixteen-sixty-five—was only her garbled way of saying "poor Boyse, poor Boyse," referring to the father. I have much to answer for, Madam, in my being so heavy-witted.'

His wife regarded him kindly and spoke soothingly.

'At the least, Sir, you had no incertainty at the end of it.'

Man's face wore a sheepish look.

'Not after,' he said in a low voice, 'not after I had the Drury Lane beggar select Christopher Boyse from a crowd in the street.'

Then Sarah Man laughed.

Later, Toby called from the bedroom for a cup of water. Sarah went in, and Man could hear her mumbling a quick story.

When she returned to her chair, she could sense that he had something to tell her.

'Is there more, husband?'

Man took a deep breath.

'Christopher Boyse has a son—or, rather, a boy.'

He had not wanted to tell her, but now he decided that she, too, should know the whole of the story.

Afterwards, she seemed to be smaller in appearance than usual.

'And when the father hangs, what will become of the son?'

Man was staring into the failing fire.

'He will probably continue sitting at the window, not moving, waiting for his father to return.'

And then, looking at his wife's face, he wished he had not said that.

CHAPTER 9

Man had been wrong so many times before that it did not matter much to him if he were wrong again. This time, at least, no harm had been done to anyone; if anything had been damaged, it was Man's pride. Evidently, he did not understand people as well as he sometimes thought he did.

He had been wrong, first, about Christopher Boyse. He had supposed that the man would submit to questioning with a dull, obstinate silence and that only the severest and most prolonged coercion would manage to elicit a complete confession.

And Boyse had, at the start, refused to plead guilty to the murder of Geoffrey Stannard and to the probable abduction of Nancy Flanner. Man had been present at the Sessions House and had watched his face—calm, seemingly unconcerned, still twitching his head to one side as if to listen for the boy who was sitting not far away in a room in Shoe Lane. It was then that Man pitied him the most, for he knew that Boyse would be desperate not to plead guilty for fear of having what little property he had confiscated by the Crown. Boyse seemed to care little for his wife, but the boy must not be left penniless.

The condemned did not show the slightest tremor, even when the awful sentence was read aloud:

That the prisoner be sent to the place from whence he came, and that he be put into a mean house, stopt from any light; and that he be laid upon his back, with his body bare, saving something to cover his privy parts: That his arms shall be stretched forth with a cord, the one to one side of the prison, the other to the other side of the prison; and in like manner shall his legs be us'd: And that upon his body shall be laid as much iron and stone as he can bear, and more; and the first day shall he have 3 morsels of barley bread, and the next day, shall he drink thrice of the water in the next channel to the prison door, but no spring, or fountain water: And this shall be his punishment till he dies.

If the deprivation of food and water meant anything to Christopher Boyse, he gave no indication of it. Man himself felt a vague sensation of watching a process come to its long-awaited conclusion.

It shocked and disturbed Man, when he learned that Boyse had named only two as friends to accompany him to the Press Yard: George Man and Taylor Hoole. It was not the first time a condemned prisoner had requested that Man be present, but somehow he had not expected it from Boyse. In some strange way, Man felt honoured and moved, as if Boyse had singled him out as one of the few who could understand him.

Man had never had much stomach for the Press Yard: the cold gloom of the place, the terrible weights methodically laid one by one on the heavy board set across the prisoner's chest, the straining for breath and the hollow groaning, and then the streams of dark blood from nose and mouth. Many confessed, but many did not; and most were a long time in dying.

At last, when they had stretched out Boyse's arms and legs and fixed the board on top of his thin chest, Man could see the beginnings of a real fear in his eyes. After the first three iron cylinders had been laid on — grotesque enlargements of those used on the shopkeeper's scales — Boyse's breath came as a tightened, rasping wail. The lips were drawn back in an ugly grin, and the limbs cramped against the tension of the cords. Man could not look away, and his own breathing seemed laboured and shallow.

Why did Christopher Boyse relent at the addition of only the sixth or seventh weight? Was it because Man had crouched down close to his ear and whispered:

'I will see to the boy.'

In his confession, Boyse described the events surrounding the murder of Geoffrey Stannard much as Man had guessed them to be. But the watchman had been badly mistaken in his assessment of the relationship between Boyse and the girl, Nancy Flanner. They had known each other well, not just for a few months before the murder, but for a full year. Boyse now talked of her with a note of affection and longing in his voice, as if she were a promise of youth come to renew his final years.

And the girl, for her part, had not tried to betray Boyse by stealing the manuscript memoirs from his home and trying to dispose of them at the receiver's in the Little Sanctuary. It was Boyse himself who, alarmed at the watchman's conversation with the girl in the chandler's shop, had sent her out with the papers to try to get the highest price she could for them. He had not wanted to implicate her any more than he already had, but he knew that her familiarity with such dealings was far greater than his own. When he had learned that the manuscript could not profitably and safely be sold, he had fallen back on his original design of publishing it under his own name and hoping for the best. And, again because of Man's persistent searching, Boyse had sent Nancy Flanner away before she could be questioned again.

This was one aspect of his work that had always intrigued and frustrated Man more than anything else: that for any given sequence of human actions, when seen from the outside, at least two—and very often more— interpretations could be imagined, each one apparently as accurate and meaningful as any other. The indeterminacy of the truth many times extended even to those people who were themselves directly involved.

A warrant was issued against Nancy Flanner. And again, as if Boyse assumed the watchman to have some special understanding of the situation, he refused to reveal the whereabouts of the girl to anyone except George Man.

Towards the end of February, Man was walking

leisurely down the tree-lined Mall on the north side of the
Canal in St James's Park. It was early in the morning; the
weather was cold, but clear. Man had wanted to make a
detour round the south-east end of the Canal, through
Duck Island and the Decoy, to see how that one crane was
faring—the one with the broken leg which had been
fitted with a jointed wooden leg fashioned by some sailor.
Man liked to watch the casual courage of the bird, which
seemed to have accepted its infirmity as something of a
natural change. But today he had to hurry: he did not
want to miss the coming in of the milkmaids from the
country.

As he continued down the Mall, he could hear some
shouting, mingled with a few curses, echoing from the
long Pelemele Alley on his right. A few eager men were
already at play. Their voices carried far through the fresh
air.

Even before he had reached the open space in front of
Buckingham House, Man could hear the rhythmic
commotion of the marching Horse and Foot Guards.
Even at this early hour, a score or more of people had
gathered to admire the scarlet coats and the flashing
guns. At the near edge of the crowd, Man noticed a pretty
young girl who was standing with a small-built man. She
was leaning her body against his and gesturing towards
the passing Guards.

Suddenly, without warning or provocation, a private
Foot detached himself from the ranks and ran over
towards the girl and the man. He obviously did not take
any time to speak, but immediately swung his arm about
and slapped the girl full in the face. She swayed against
her companion for support.

The watchman could then hear the sound of the two
men's voices raised in argument, although he could not
make out their words. The outline of the soldier's body
seemed to change; he reared back and brought his

musket up above his shoulders; then he struck the small man in the head with the stock-end of his gun. The dull sound of the blow came clearly through the air. The man lay crumpled and still on the ground.

It had all happened so quickly, so unexpectedly, that Man was caught off-balance. He watched the scene from a distance, as if it were a puppet-play: the sounds muted and indistinct, the movements sudden and unconnected. Already the officers of the Horse had surrounded the soldier, and Man could see a couple of his fellow watchmen closing in from the opposite direction. There was nothing left for him to do.

A few yards behind Man, a milkmaid had run up to see the trouble, leaving her pail standing next to an old man who was drinking a penny mug of warm milk. She was wearing a simple country dress that looked as if it had been passed from woman to woman. Her face was fresh and happy, and she walked with an unconscious clumsiness that seemed simple and contented.

Man came up silently behind Nancy Flanner as she was returning to her pail.

'You have been long missed, girl.'

She turned about at the sound of his voice, and Man could not say if she looked fearful or relieved.

'How did you find me, Sir?'

'He told me.'

She must have guessed from the first, for her relaxed posture did not change; but her hands, which had been raised, fell to her sides at rest.

'Might I finish my work? The milk will frost over.'

Man stood beside her as she ladled out the foaming milk to passing ladies and children. He bought a cup for himself and felt the thick milk warm his entire body. He looked through the trees at Rosamond's Pond and smiled. He could never see it without thinking of a windy afternoon years ago, when he had pulled another milkmaid, wet and laughing, from the water. And, as always, he thought of Sarah.

A quarter of an hour later the girl and the watchman were walking together by the Canal. Man was carrying the empty pail.

'What were your plans, then?'

Nancy Flanner looked at him shyly. She seemed to Man to have outgrown much of the servility which he had seen in her only last fall.

'There is a farmhouse that wants buying. 'Tis small, but exceeding clean. A bit of land, some few cows . . .'

'And what was to be done with Mistress Boyse?'

She did not answer, only looked away and shivered—but it could have been the cold.

Then Man knew that Christopher Boyse's plans were much more complicated than he had suspected, that he was looking towards the future as well as the past.

He glanced down at the girl's slightly protruding belly and felt glad, although he could not have said exactly why. He felt a deep and gratifying sense of continuation.

Sarah had turned Man out of the house, telling him that if he wanted to be so moody and grumbling, he could just take himself out and be so in the streets. He was, she said, distracting Toby from his lessons.

It was not his work which was irritating him; that went on much as it always did. Somewhat better, in fact: the wild gangs in the St Giles area had been dispersed, and most of Man's nights were quiet and uneventful.

Nancy Flanner had pleaded her belly and been transported to Virginia.

Christopher Boyse had been hanged at Tyburn before what was to some a distressingly small and unenthusiastic crowd. The weather could have had something to do with it: it was cold and rainy, with a wind that blew into the spectators' faces and shut their eyes. Boyse twisted at the end of the rope for fifteen minutes, strangling and choking, finally experiencing the kind of suffering which he had so dreaded in the Press Yard. At last Taylor Hoole stepped forward and clasped the man about the legs, adding his own weight to shorten the agony. Man was not there.

Even Boyse's son had, pathetically, not given Man much trouble. He had simply refused to eat, in spite of the watchman's grim efforts and the leaden silence of the wife. The boy had thrashed about in his chair like a mortally wounded animal and had died a few weeks after his father.

So here Man was, standing in front of the Heath house in Drury Lane on an overcast, blustering afternoon. He had come to talk to Mother Emeny one last time. He could not have explained it to anyone, not even to Sarah, but he felt that he had to tell the old woman what had happened and why. She was the only one left who had been present both at the beginning and at the end of a sixty-year-long process.

In the house, nothing had changed since Man's first visit. Alan Heath was away from home again, tending to his stall in St Martin's Court. Amelia Heath was still bent over her books. And Mother Emeny could still be heard mumbling and wandering in her memories.

This time, Man thought that the old woman seemed somewhat more aware of his presence, even more coherent in her disconnected murmurings. He was still unnerved by the clouded, opaque stare of her useless eyes. Unlike many of the blind, she held her eyes open wide, never blinking, the shrivelled and parchment-thin lids drawn back painfully into the skull. As Man had learned at his previous meeting with her, Mother Emeny was not completely stone-deaf. She seemed to be able to hear what was spoken clearly and forcibly straight into her ear. But she had become so accustomed to the voice of Amelia

Heath that the younger woman had come to serve as translator, not for Man alone, but for her husband and for others as well. And even then, there seemed to be some internal dissociation between sense and understanding that made any true communication impossible.

Gradually, with patience and persistence, Man was able to relay to the old woman what he had learned about the history of the house next door. He told her everything, in abbreviated form, about Geoffrey Stannard and the Boyse family, both in the past and in the present. He omitted nothing, including even the recent deaths of Christopher Boyse and of the idiot son, Samuel. He wanted most to try to make her understand the reasons which lay behind the sequence of events: Stannard's fears of death and poverty, Boyse's lifelong bitterness and hopelessness.

At the mention of the name 'Samuel,' the grandmother appeared to retreat for a time into herself, as if she were reviewing a part of the past that had been called forth by association. Man imagined that, within the uncontrollable welter of her mind, Mother Emeny was trying to piece together the information which he had given her with what she could remember and with what she had all but forgotten. It seemed a long and hurtful effort: Man could read in the old woman's face the changes from confusion through disbelief to her own kind of shadowy comprehension.

And then she began to cry.

Even Amelia Heath could not understand it. The old lady had never carried on so, not even at the deaths of her own husband and children. Mother Emeny sat unmoving, sobbing and moaning. Nothing that either Man or Amelia Heath could do helped to calm her. Man thought she would never stop.

She began to speak, in a voice choked by phlegm.

'All . . . for nothing . . . all.'

Man bent forward towards her ear until the fine white hairs brushed against his lips.

'What was it? What was all for nothing?'

'Henry . . . Henry told me it . . .'

Amelia Heath whispered to Man that this was the name of the grandmother's husband.

Man gently coaxed her on.

'Henry told you . . .'

The old woman's weeping increased.

'Samuel . . . poor Samuel . . . must stay . . . must stay behind . . .'

The rest of Mother Emeny's words were as indistinct as the first haphazard mouthings of a baby. When Man had finally deciphered enough to understand, he sat back slowly and closed his eyes.

As he was leaving, he stopped for a moment before the still-unoccupied house next door. The house in which Nancy Flanner had conceived, while an old man sat struggling for life downstairs: the house which young Geoffrey Stannard had seen as the beginning of his rise to fortune and power: the house where Samuel Boyse had died alone—not of his injuries or of starvation, but of the plague.

All for nothing.

It took a longer time than usual for Man to make his way back to Ironmonger Row. Sarah could not be cross with him now; his churlish mood had passed, leaving him solemn and thoughtful. For once, he took little notice of the varied sights and sounds of the streets.

As he neared the turning into his own street, he saw three men ahead of him who were walking in the same direction. One, the most gaunt of the three, he recognized as Taylor Hoole; the second, larger and with a rolling gait, was Captain Thomas Coram; the third he did not know.

★

Walking between the two men towards Ironmonger Row, Taylor Hoole was hoping fervently that he was doing the right thing.

He should have first come alone, he knew that now. He should have given them the bad news gradually, with a gentle and unemotional explanation, instead of bringing it in person to their door. Sarah would be devastated; Man, too, probably. Hoole dreaded what was to come and wished it were already over.

It had been last October that he had been sitting with Man over two steaming dishes in a nearly empty coffee-house in Addle Hill. Man had had a favour to ask of him. He had just learned that, in 1665, the then-unknown mother and son from Drury Lane had removed with the Heath family to a ship in the river to shelter from the expected onslaught of the Great Plague. Could the name or the owners of that one ship still be traced? If so, then there might be some hope of discovering what had become of the mother and the boy or—at the very least—the name. There was small chance of success after so many years, but he was desperate to try everything. And Man's own time was so taken up with the present-day events in Drury Lane and with the boy at home that he felt that he needed as much help as he could get.

Hoole had been anxious to do anything he could. He felt himself personally involved, not only because it was he who had found Geoffrey Stannard's shrunken body—a moment that continued to revisit him in his dreams—but also because of the sad, painful thoughts of his own father which he still carried about with him like an open sore.

As they were finishing the last of their coffees, he noticed that his friend had kept glancing impatiently towards the door. And when a certain man had come in—a burly gentleman with a full face and a fine sword—the watchman had at once stood up to motion him over to their table. Evidently the two of them had already arranged to meet here.

Taylor Hoole and Captain Thomas Coram had taken to each other from the first. They were near the same age, and they shared an interest both in religious controversies and in public works. Hoole liked the Captain's gruff kindliness: he called him one of the decentest men he had ever met.

From that day onward the two men had spent a good deal of their time together — poring over moulded records of ownership, studying written accounts of the Plague Year which pertained mainly to maritime activities, talking to dozens of retired seamen whose memories were as worn as their faces. Nothing, finally, had come of it; the records were sketchy and chaotic, and many of the pages had crumbled into dust in their hands. But a strong bond had grown up between the two men, one which reached beyond the futility of their efforts.

At the beginning of April the Captain had come on a surprise visit to Taylor Hoole's room near St John's Gate. It was an evening of high winds and fitful rain, and the watchman was putting on an extra pair of stockings before going out to work.

The Captain had crossed the room, holding out before him a rough news-sheet, one that circulated among those in the shipping trade. His hard, thick finger had been pointed at an advertisement:

> Mr Paul Childers begs leave to inform all who may have known of him before his enforced absence in America that he is now returned and desires any serious information that can be secured concerning whichever members of his poor family may have the good fortune to survive: daughter Roxana or sons Philip or Toby. Inquiries to be left at the Cut Mast Coffee House next to the Trig Stairs.

✦

The Captain had gone to meet Paul Childers and could give a good report of him. He had been a luckless greengrocer whose prodigal habits had attracted the attention of the press-gang. After somehow winning his liberty off the shores of the American Colonies, he had immediately resumed his reckless life where he had left it off. Only the chance news of his wife's death had succeeded in sobering him to a changed way of living. He had started a modest trading in Virginia tobacco, saved his money wisely, and taken a new wife. But the woman grew lonely for the London she had known as a girl; and they had returned to settle in her father's old house and to search for the remnants of his family.

Paul Childers already had learned of the loss of his two elder children. But the Captain had remembered Toby from his visit to Man's: Coram was one of those rare adults to whom children do not appear all alike. Now he was come to Taylor Hoole first, to ask his help in carrying the delicate business through.

And here Hoole was, almost at Man's house, and sick with the worry that he was making a mess of the whole affair. He looked sideways at the tobacco trader: a small, wiry man who wore the ravages of his former errors in his lined face and across his rounded shoulders, yet who seemed now to carry himself with gentleness and confidence. He would make a good father, reflected Hoole, this man who had won out against himself.

When they reached the street door next to the bake-shop above which the Mans lived, Taylor Hoole heard his name called out and turned to see George Man edging his way between a soldier and a girl. The watchman came up to them and looked from one to the other, waiting for an introduction to Paul Childers, but Hoole spoke first.

'It has to do with the boy, Toby.'

Hoole was watching Man's face closely. He had looked somewhat troubled and dispirited, when he had first come to join them, but now he seemed silently to strengthen himself. His face hardened, and he fixed a curious gaze upon Paul Childers.

Upstairs, Sarah was helping the boy to read. They were sitting together near the low fire, the boy's small head resting securely against the woman's shoulder.

Taylor Hoole stood shifting his weight from one foot to the other. It was his work now to make the introductions, but he could not find the words. And all the while he could feel Man watching him and waiting patiently.

Sarah looked politely at the three men, nodding towards the newcomer, but not understanding. She had a welcoming smile on her face that made Hoole feel weak.

The boy stood at her side, looking mildly bored. He obviously wished these intruders would hurry about their business and be gone. This was his home now, he had thrived in its warmth, and he was jealous of its security.

Sarah turned towards her husband.

'Coffee, Mr Man, or some ale perhaps . . .'

In answer, Man moved reluctantly towards her and the boy.

'Toby, I believe you are needed by your father.'

Hoole listened for the quaver he had expected in his friend's voice, but could hear none. Man's profile showed nothing, neither joy for the child nor sorrow for himself.

The Captain grumbled deep in his chest, and Paul Childers coughed uneasily, as the boy stared at him in sudden fear. Hoole himself felt numb and tired.

Only Sarah could speak. Her voice sounded dull with pain.

'But who is this man, George? Some foul Spiriter come to take yet another son away from us? That would be hard, George, that would be too hard.'

Man went up to his wife and laid a hand across her back.

'He is Paul Childers. He claims what is by law and by nature a part of him.'

Son and father stared at one another across the quiet room.

'We have borne worse, Sarah,' Man reminded her. 'And this is for the boy.'

She made a last desperate effort.

'And how are we to truly know he is the father?'

Paul Childers spoke up almost apologetically:

'He was but an infant, when I was taken. But there is a mark . . .' touching behind his own left ear.

Sarah ran from the room, the boy following.

For the next few minutes Man hurried about, arranging chairs and bringing out their best cups. He poured from a treasured bottle of brandy that Hoole knew he had been rationing for nearly a year. Gradually, the tension in the room relaxed, and the men were able to talk and smoke.

Paul Childers told Man his story, leaving out nothing of his own past mistakes and failings. He was settled now in Westminster and eager to resume his trading in tobacco. It would be rough going at first, he thought, not knowing anyone here who was in the business.

'Just there, Sir, I might be able to aid you in some small way,' Man spoke round the stem of his pipe. 'There's one I know in the City, one I met through my friend, Mr Defoe, who himself has done a piece of trading in his day. The first is active still, and I should think he would be happy to direct you. He's a fine sort.'

Paul Childers acknowledged his indebtedness and reminded Man that the watchman and his wife would be made welcome in his home at any time.

The windows were beginning to grey with twilight when Sarah and the boy came back into the room. The boy carried a bundle of the clothes which Sarah had made him. Hoole was relieved to see that she was now more composed, even happy.

Man said that he might have just enough time before sunset to accompany Paul Childers into the City to introduce him to the tobacco trader. Taylor Hoole and the Captain were assigned to walk Sarah and the boy to his new home in Westminister. A mood of quiet thoughtfulness hung over everyone as they made ready to leave, although Hoole noticed that the boy still looked at his father with a dubious mistrust and still stayed near to Sarah.

They separated in Old Street. And from this afternoon Taylor Hoole was to remember most two distinct moments, two balanced images.

The first was when Man was about to walk off towards the City with Paul Childers. The watchman had reached out and lightly caressed the boy's fair hair with his fingertips. Then he had turned away.

And the second was when Hoole had looked back at the receding figures of Man and the tobacco trader, both made vague by the gathering dusk. The father had seemed slight and frail compared to the solid bulk of the watchman. And then, just for a moment, Man had placed his hand against the back of his companion, as if to help him along.